4th Sunday
in the dirty
By
Kent Hughes

Mike Parker, Editor

This book is a work of fiction. Names of characters, places and incidents are products of the author's imagination or are used fictitiously. Any resemblance to actual events or locales or persons living, or dead is entirely coincidental.

I dedicate this book to my dad, Jesse Hughes senior: I loved your sense of humor and your great story telling. I remember...Theresa, Jesse Jr. Elevese, Jennifer, Sheila Sherick, and me of course... sitting around drawn to your every word... and asking mom was it true...Miss you Cap!

To Mike Parker: It's funny how, without knowing, a word of encouragement given at a precise moment can change the life of a passer-by. Glad I passed your way. To Shelia Williams, Elevese McLean, Jennifer Sykes, Theresa Figgs, Dora Hughes, Thanks for your input and for being the ladies you all are. To Kenesha, Chasity, and Tiamia Hughes: The gift was passed on to you girls so use it. To Mike and P.J… you know what's up keep striving for greatness!

To the two most important ladies in my life, Maiseville G. Hughes and Tiffnii Hughes: I simply love ya'll.

And to all the women that I've known in life: I've listened to each and every one of you. Believe me, I did. That's how I was able to write this…LOL

Well – maybe I went deaf on a few.

4th Sunday

in the dirty

Table of Contents

4th Sunday

in the

Dirty

Chair of despair

I placed the chair of despair
Into the dark corner of my mind
I sat and stared into this light...that
Once... I could never find
The light projected all the mistakes
Of my unconscious yesterdays
Yet... I studied the light very carefully
To understand why mistakes were made
When I...
Removed the chair of despair
From the corner... which was dark no more
My only regret is...
I should have sat
In the corner long before
Kent Hughes

PREFACE

This is the first edition of the F.S.I.T.D(4th Sunday in the Dirty) series. I wrote this not having a clue as to what I was doing. It was my first time attempting to put my imagination on paper, and for some reason I knew it was meant to happen. As I begin putting the outline together my confidence began to build and the next thing, I knew, I had a story that would change my life... in the world of writing... forever.

I had written many poems but nothing of this magnitude, so I was excited to get started on the first page. But after writing the first line I froze...went blank...nothing followed. My brain was broken...and I was left wondering just how I was now going to pull this off. I started to read the first line over and over and over again... and each time I read it I got absolutely...nothing. Sooo... I gracefully close my little composition book, I didn't have a computer at the time, and walked away.

It took me about two days and suddenly it hit me... while I was lying in bed. And boy! Did I get excited... again, because I knew for a fact it was going to work.

Because I grew up with four sisters... and I am a mama's boy and the fact that I had funny aunts... and most of my closest friends were females, I have heard some of the craziest stories. I decided to write this story as a female narrating and/or telling her side of the story... and trust me Beatrice Harold did not let us down.

Growing up in the sixties, seventies, and early eighties, in Camden, for me, was a blast. I can only speak for myself and my family when I tell you that... we had so much fun, and the love for each other is unmatchable. Even to this day, we get together and it's just like we never missed a beat with the storytelling and reminiscing about the good old days.

This story takes place in the little, small, one stop light, town of Camden North Carolina that I call home. When you read this story, I am hoping you can feel the love, the joy and yes, the sometimes pain that the Harold family endures as they navigate through their journey in life. 4th Sunday is indeed a fictional story nothing about it is true, but when I tell you it was so much fun to write, believe me it was. My advice to you … get in a cozy spot where you will not be disturbed and get ready. Beatrice Harold has a lot on her mind, and she is ready to tell you what lead up to, and… how it went down on "4th Sunday in the Dirty"!!!

PS: My fans would often ask me where is part one…because I put out **Three Lies pt. 2** then **Pinch Gut Road pt. 3** before **4th Sunday.**

I put **4th Sunday** out last because when I wrote **Three Lies** everyone wanted a sequel. I began writing **Pinch Gut Road,** (never publishing it) to piggyback off **Three Lies** …**4th Sunday** was an entirely different story, yet most of the characters are in all three books. When I decided to put the 3 books out again some 15 years later, it only made sense for me to start out with **Three Lies,** followed by **Pinch Gut Road…**and even though I wrote '**4th Sunday in the Dirty** first. I had to add a few lines to '**4th Sunday**' to make it tie in a little better with the other two and well I guess the rest is history.

Thank you all for your patience and thank you even more for your support…**One Luv**

CHAPTER 1

THE WORD NOT THE MAN

My marriage was folding like a crisp one-hundred-dollar bill in a pimp's money clip.

I hadn't been moist since the day I first met my dear sweet husband Harry, and although he was not part of the moisture building inside me, I was dying to release and relieve myself of some unwanted stress.

The release date is tonight, and my reliever...Tavone McKnight.

I spent all day getting ready for this moment, starting maybe even in my sleep the night before, and I was sure this was the right move to make. To make sure this would go off without any mistakes, I called my best friend, in the whole wide world, Teeny Baby, asking if she would meet me at Little Times... only the sexiest lingerie store in Camden, North Carolina.

Teeny Baby not only was my best friend, but she was also the sneakiest and biggest hoe in Camden.

At one time I thought she was messing around with my Harry, but I knew Harry didn't have the type of money it takes to what she calls "break her back," so I gave it little thought.

Plus, Harry didn't like her that much anyway. He says, "She stinks."

Only because she wears too much perfume sometimes.

But…Today I wasn't going to think about my husband because I had other things on my mind and Harry was not going to be in my zone during this touch down.

It was about noon when I met Teeny Baby.

The first thing out of Teeny Baby's mouth was, "Are you really going to break him off a piece, girl?"

Without hesitation I asked, "Is a Donkey … Kong? Is a Go … Rilla"?

Teeny Baby laughed and said, "I don't know. I haven't tried one of those yet, but I will put that on my list of things to screw."

"Beatrice," she asked with what we country folks call a shit-eating grin, "why haven't you done something about your bird a long time ago? Hell! I could hear the damned thing chirping every time we went to the mall for our morning walk."

"The same reason those blind cats follow you when we go for our evening walk down your dirt path," I replied. "It's a shame you have got those blind cats thinking that you are a walking Red Lobster."

Teeny Baby and I were probably the craziest two women in Camden and like few friendships we would say almost anything to each other and had few secrets.

The first thing she picked out was a tiger stripped coochie excess panty and bra negligee.

"Teeny Baby," I said, "you have got to be kidding me. I want to have sex with the man, not give him a heart attack. This man is soon to be an ordained minister. I don't want to scare the man to death."

11

"Yeah! You might scare the devil out of him," Teeny Baby said. "You know he's going straight to hell if he breaks your back tonight. I'm a little fast and even I know you don't suppose to play with God."

I think Teeny Baby was just a little bit jealous, but not of Tavone. But because of the fact she hadn't had herself a man of the cloth yet.
***

Down South preachers are known to make good money if they can find a church and he was already guaranteed one as soon as he finished school. The New Shady Creek Baptist Church in Camden had offered him a position, the church where I just happened to be a member.

***

We picked out a beautiful laced out white negligee with a matching see through gown. I even got me some of those slippers that looked like pumps with the little fur laced on top. They looked something like Cinderella's glass slippers and after all I was going to have a ball tonight.

We spent about two hours in Little Times trying out different types and styles.

Teeny Baby wanted to make sure she had a lot of input in what I decided to buy because when I was done doing my business, I couldn't keep the evidence, so I had to give the negligee to her. She even tells me to take it off before I get started and don't put it back on when I finished. I guess I should take an extra pair of thongs. I know that sound a little nasty but ya'll just don't know Teeny Baby.

After we left Little Times, we went to The Bath and Body Shop to get some smell good. I already knew what I wanted, so we only spent a few minutes in there, and it was on to Wal-mart.

We didn't get anything from Wal-mart; it was just our routine to go there whenever we were out. It was something like a fellowship-meeting place. Just like the friends on the commercials.

We started running short on time, so Teeny Baby said, "We better split because I have business of my own to take care of."

"Split! Girl, you haven't seen a split since high school," I said.

"What-ever," she said, laughed and waved good-bye, quickly reminding me to call her ASAP when it's a done deal.

* * *

Being it was already about 3:30 pm and my rendezvous with destiny was at seven, I rushed home to cook dinner for my Harry.

Harry was going to watch the NBA championship tonight, which gave me a free night out with the girls. At least that's what he thought.

He's always watching basketball with Bucky, Knotts, Junior Cefuss and that loudmouth ass Lips.

I don't know any of their real names and didn't care to know. All I knew was it was my chance to get the hell out of dodge and do my "thang."

If I sound a little nonchalant it's simply because on our first anniversary my beloved husband Harry gave me gonorrhea. No time was the right time for a disease, but on my first anniversary? I could've died; better yet, I could have killed him instead.

With counseling and two months of living with my Ma Elsie dodging snuff, spit cups and curfews, I decided to carry my ass back home and just keep my bird in its cage for a while and make Harry suffer. He begged me to come back home, so I figured if I was going to be there, he was going to be miserable.

But tonight, I'm going to let my caged bird sing.

I've never given Harry a reason to believe I was ready to explode inside because I always pretend to have nothing to do with sex – ever, but deep down inside I was even thinking of letting him have a little something-something, but I was afraid I'd get a flash back and cut off his little friend.

* * *

I took a shower and got dressed.

On the way out the door Harry yelled out, sounding like God speaking to Moses at the burning bush, "Don't be out all night."

"Yes, dear," I sarcastically said and rushed out to my car.

On my way to the Colonial Inn, about 30 minutes away from my house in Camden, all I could do was think about how good it would feel to have my body licked down from the waist down. I wanted to moan like a virgin being touch for the very first time. And like Betty Wright, tonight is the night.

* * *

Tavone was a very nice gentleman. I met him when I was attending Elizabeth State University in Elizabeth City, NC. We were in the marching band at State. I was a senior and he was a junior. We never really carried a conversation, but occasionally, he would come over and sit beside the band members.

He would start to preach and carrying on.

Most of the time we would just pick fun at him. Like the day after practice, it was hot as the devil; Tavone asked a couple of the band mates, "If the world ended tomorrow, where would ya'll end up, heaven or hell?"

One of the guys said they didn't know, but wherever they ended up, it would be nice to know it wasn't in Elizabeth City.

I had to put my two cents.

"Yeah, and if it's where you are, I hope you leave that trumpet 'cause you sound like shit."

He was very easy going so he just laughed along with us. Tavone is about 6'3, a little lighter than my taste, but he was fine as hell.

A few years later I would often see him at church every now and then… and to top it off he wasn't married at the time… Although I was.

Harry didn't go to church, so I would fine myself going alone most of the time. I saw Tavone at church on 4th Sunday…I hadn't seen him since our old college days and somehow, we sparked a conversation. I began to tell him what's been happening in my life since last we saw each other. Soon after, we would see each other most Sundays at church. After a while I went only hoping to see him.

15

One Sunday Tavone asked me would I like to go out to dinner. At first, I was a little pessimistic. Then I thought, "What the hell.? Being that we were from a small town, we decided to meet in Virginia Beach at the Olive Garden.

Soon we were meeting all over Virginia: Norfolk, Chesapeake, Newport News, and Hampton. Once we made it as far as Richmond. Richmond was a close call. I almost got caught in a lie because I had gotten home so late.

It was about 11 pm when Tavone and I arrived back in Camden and about 12:30 am when I got home.

Who else but Harry met me at the door sounding like God when he was talking to Moses at the burning bush.

"Damn! Where have you been – Heaven somewhere? I know church service ain't that long. What did the preacher do, read the whole Bible?"

Before I could answer Teeny Baby called.

Harry picked up the phone.

Teeny Baby was asking him had I made it home yet, explaining to Harry we had been drinking a little, and she wanted to make sure I was safe.

"Yea, she made it home alright, but you need to drink by yourself," I heard Harry say. "Beatrice is married and got a man at home."

He then slammed the phone down like he was trying to tear it up.

I asked who it was.

"It was Teeny Baby calling to make sure you got home safe," he said.

Harry asked was I a drunk now, and I sung to him, "How dry I am." He laughed and went back into the living room to finish watching basketball. His favorite team was playing, so I guess if I had gone in their butt naked, he would have argued for a few minutes and then gone back to watching that stupid game.

Because Harry never went to church with me, he calls me a religious freak with a freaky friend (Teeny Baby, of course).

Remember Teeny Baby is a sneaky chick, and when she saw my car turn at Belcross, she figured I needed a little help. Lucky, I had a blue Hawaiian or two at dinner to compliment the lie she told Harry. Man! She's good.

I ended that little sneaky thing because I knew I had something good at home and I wasn't going to have sex with Tavone anyway...I guess I was just missing something at home at the time and thought I needed a friend.

Little did I know years later I'd be giving up the goods to him.

Okay back to the story...

   * * *

As I turned in to the Colonial Inn, I saw Tavone and he was there waiting and ready.

For some reason my knees started knocking together like a monkey chewing bobbed wire and I was sweating like a pig turning on a roast rack. My heart was pounding like the Grinch trying to keep the sled from falling over the cliff, while the palms of my hands were sweaty as if I were washing clothes by hand.

Maybe I should have parked in a handicap parking space or had him to meet me with a wheelchair because there was no way I was going to make it to the door on my own. My nerves were shot to pieces.

Somehow, I managed to make it to the room.

We had planned this for quite some time, and from the looks of it, he was more than ready.

I walked into the door like Carrie when she was at the prom on stage covered in pig blood.

He had all the right tools and like a 2x4 I knew I was going to get nailed, so I braced myself for the pounding.

17

It was about twelve o'clock. Time, for some reason, was slipping faster than I was.

We did something I hadn't done after sex in a long time. Talked.

The conversation started off with, "So what's next?"

Tavone told me he thinks he was in love (one of those loves you're in after good sex). I just smiled and agreed.

I asked, "How was I?"

"Warm, soft, gentle, and slow – just the way I like it," he said.

I already knew my bird was good because it had been marinating for over a year or more.

"Come on now," I said with a little teenage girl's charm.

He just smiled.

"Would I lie?"

"I trust you, Rev," I replied, and he said, "Do you trust the word or the man?" and I told him, "I trust both."

It was soon time to leave, so I fixed my hair and freshened up a little remembering not to put on the lingerie. I placed it back into the bag for Teeny Baby.

Imagine: I was still thinking about that crazy girl after all this and couldn't wait to call her ASAP.

We soon kissed and departed with me hoping this wasn't the last time I was going to play "break back" like my friend and get my "back broke" again as soon as possible.

On the ride back home, the song came on ("If loving you is wrong, I don't want to be right") and it flushed any guilt I had right down the toilet.

I started having anxiety attacks anticipating arriving home and walking through the door and greeting my husband after a night of wild sex, in which he had no part. The closer I came to the house the heavier my breathing became. By the time I pulled onto North River Road, I was hyperventilating like someone had a gun to my head asking for a million dollars knowing I didn't have a dime in my pocket. As the house came into view, I somehow started to imagine hearing Harry ask the big question: "Have you been cheating on me?"

And I was going answer him with that shit eating grin.

"You damned right"

Knowing how scared and nervous I was, I'd rather for the guy with the imaginary gun asking me for a million dollars to just shoot me before I would answer Harry with a "you damned right." As a matter of fact, if he asks me something like that, I'll probably go straight into a coma.

As I turned in the driveway, I blew my horn for one of Harry's friends to move his car. Lips walked out with his loud ass mouth and said, "If it were me, your ass would have to sleep in the car coming in this late."

"If you were Harry, I would sleep in the car every damned night," I said to Lips. "Now shut your big ass lips up and move that riding mower you call a car." I had to get one more joke in on Lips so I told him he would be better off putting some helium in those big ass lips and float around in stead of wasting precious fuel.

"Yo' mama," Lips simply said.

I guess he got joked about his lips so much, "yo' mama" was his only way out.

When I walked in the house, it was smoked out. I could have sworn that I told Harry not to smoke in the house. My first instinct was to go in acting the fool and kick every body's butt out of my house including crazy

Harry. I decided tonight I wouldn't have cared if the whole entire house burned down to a crisp as long as no one was hurt.

I must have forgot to wipe that grin off my face because as soon as I walked in the living room Harry said, "What? Have you won the lottery tonight."

After what I've experience tonight, I felt like Ed McMahon had personally come to my house to hand me a check.

I explained to Harry that I didn't win the lottery, but I did find out I still had It. "It," Harry said with that voice. "What the hell is a - It?"

I explained to him, a lot of men were asking me to dance and trying to get my phone number.

I got so many pulls that I felt like I was butt naked walking through the club.

"Pulls? Pulls what" …asked Harry

And here I go explaining again… Pulls are when you are looked up and down and guys are coming on to you like flies to an outhouse, trying to get a conversation and some cheap lay.

Harry said he heard enough, but his friends, on the other hand, seemed to be very interested.

Bucky asked what club I went to, Junior Cefuss asked was Teeny Baby there and Knotts told me I looked good enough to eat.

I answered each question in the order in which they were asked.

"Bucky, I went to the Hutt."

"Junior Cefuss, yes, Teeny Baby was there."
I then made remarks to Knotts' statement.

"Knotts, you couldn't bite into a wet marshmallow with those rotten ass teeth."

I then turned like a runway model and walked out thinking to myself, "Where in the hell did my husband get those ugly ass friends from?"

Harry says he keeps ugly friends so he wouldn't have to worry about me trying to push up on one of them. I guess he had a point because I would rather chew off one of my arms than to give one of them a hug.

So, I think he was right on the money.

After I prepared for bed, I drowned in my lust. Shameful at times yet satisfied with the moment of pleasure.

The sad part was the lying I had to do. And I was good at it if I say so myself. Maybe this will teach Harry that there is more than the game of sports. There's also the game of love. Right now, he is losing

I picked up the phone to call Teeny Baby – ASAP, of course, but there was no answer. I left a message on her answering machine for her to call me back. I figured she was either out to the Hutt or getting her back broke and not answering her phone. Either way, she will call me as soon as she has a chance because she's got to know everything that happens.

After getting all comfortable in bed I reached on the nightstand for *Black Frame*. *Black Frame* was a book of poetry Tavone bought me when we were on one of our little get-a-ways. I loved reading this book. It was as if the poet had me in mind when he was writing it. Tavone's favorite was one called "If Asked"

If Asked

If asked... to describe my love, I'd say
Warm

Soft
Gentle
And slow
If asked... how far would I take my love... I'd say

Forever... is how far I'd go
    If asked..., how do I love thee... I couldn't even
count the ways
    I'd just...
    Hope and wish
    For a better love
    And pray
    For better days
    And if God for some reason should take us...
        Far away from here... I'd wait to find my place
    in Heaven
    Because I know I'd find you there...
    If asked...

This had to be the most beautiful thing I have ever read, at least for the moment.

Now the waiting in heaven part wasn't probably going to happen, if you know what I mean.

While I was in the room reading, I overheard Junior Cefuss asking Harry why he allowed me to go out with Teeny Baby to a club. Junior Cefuss went on to say how much of a freak Teeny Baby is and how it looked bad for a married woman to be hanging out with a nasty skank hoe like her.

I wanted to know also. I listen closely for the reasoning behind his kindness. Like always, Harry stayed cool and answered in a calm but straightforward way.

"My woman's grown," said Harry. "She comes and goes when and with who she wants."

"Soon she'll be coming with someone, and it won't be you," Junior Cefuss replied.

I knew Harry wasn't going to take that from Junior Cefuss, but surprisingly Harry just told him to watch his mouth before he will be wiping his ass off the floor.

All the guys started laughing and it was time for jokes.

"I'm screwing your wife," Bucky said to Junior Cefuss. "Did she tell you that?"

Junior Cefuss replied, "No, but she did tell me you used to come around and open Similac cans for the baby using those buck ass teeth."

The guys went on joking and playing cards. I believe Harry was thinking about what Jr. Cefuss said earlier because he wasn't talking too much after that. After eavesdropping on their little card game, I started feeling a little guilty about tonight and all the lying I had to do today to accomplish this mission.

At about 3:45 am, Harry came to bed. I was probably in my second gear of sleep. My second gear was when I could hear you talking and could answer you correctly but wouldn't remember a thing in the morning.

For some reason Harry was in a talking mood. I remembered him asking me if I still loved him. I remembered answering yes, I love you, my pooh bear. He may have asked me if I forgave him… and again, I answered with a yes, only this yes came with a "Now will you please leave me alone?"

By this time, I was fading fast, but not Harry. He continues to ask questions and for the first time I gave a wrong answer. All I heard was "Baby," and the next thing I remember was my legs so far up in the air that I could feel a cold draft between my toes from outer space. I woke to the rhythm of Harry beating my bird like the drums of an old African folk song and I was moaning like there was no tomorrow. I'll put it like this, I didn't know how much I missed my Harry until I got my third one, if you know what I mean.

I held on to my Harry and vowed to try and make this marriage work. Harry had already taken the first step by

giving me all this unwanted freedom, I pretended I needed. I guess when you are looking for an apology and don't get the one you think you deserved; you sometimes feel like you never got one.

Maybe there wasn't an apology good enough.

Maybe I should have just left him. Maybe.

Maybe.

Maybe.

I always loved my Harry; he just really messed my mind up with that crazy stunt he pulled.

For now, I'll put it all to the back burner and start over again.

It's a good thing that Harry and I finally made up because Tavone dropped a bomb on me on our last meeting, telling me he was engaged. That means he was with her the whole time he was sleeping with me. He was trying to explain to me the how's and why's, but I was so busy trying to get my marriage together that I didn't care.

Well! Maybe I was hurt just a little because I thought it was only me. I guess it turns out he was a holy asshole.

I 'm glad I used protection with him.

After Harry, I didn't trust anyone.

I found myself lying to Tavone and Harry so much that I didn't even trust me.

CHAPTER 2

PORCH DECKS AND RIVER
DAMS
**** Ten years later****

It's something about the North Carolina air, especially in Camden, preferable in the evening when the sun starts playing with the clouds dodging in and out of their fluffy heavens. The breeze starts blowing through the pine trees giving off the aroma of a freshly sprayed sky. Somehow the sun wins the game of hide and seek. Before it has a chance to play burn the skin, I manage to retrieve to my favorite spot behind the house where shade is like an outside Maytag air conditioner.

"Alex, where is your sister?" I asked.

"Riding her bike somewhere," he answered maintaining a speed on his bike that could have won at any race on the motor cross.

"Where is somewhere?" I yelled back.

"Somewhere down the road," Alex yelled back as he skids around the corner like he was some daredevil.

"You take your speed demon behind down that road and tell your sister to get her fast behind in this yard."

I didn't mind them riding their bikes as long as I could keep an eye on them. Sometimes those stray dogs would get behind you bark and growling, almost causing you to break your neck trying to get away from them. They would never bite you; only scare you enough to cause you to kill yourself.

25

Beany came riding up in the yard with her head tilted to the side like it was too heavy for her neck.

Breanna, or Beany as we called her, was about the sassiest little thing I had ever seen in my life. And what's so bad about it is she looked just like her daddy.

All five little years of her.

Believe me, there wasn't anything she didn't know, at least that's what she thought.

She told me once that she was sorry for staying in the hospital for so long, she said that she just wasn't sure if she was ready to stay here. When she told me that, I looked at her with a curious face, more like I was shocked.

"Stay where?" I asked her.

Beany then looked back.

"You know, mom, here on earth."

Now! I tell you what. I don't know how she knew all this because I never told her she was a premature baby or that she was in the hospital for six weeks after she was born, but somehow, she knew. And to make things more complicated she was only two years old when she told me this.

Ma Elsie said that she had "It".

Not the "It", I thought I had when I was at that make believed club years ago.

I'm talking about the real "It".

The "It" that Great Grandma Amy had.

"It" was the gift to see things before they happen or to see things from the future – or the past. Hell! Just see things.

I, on the other hand, didn't really believe in all that backwater crap, and if Beany ever tells me that she sees dead people, she got to get the hell out of here. Lord only knows, if she ever gets stuck in the television, she had better follow the light because the television is going straight out the window.

Now Harry, on the other hand, eats that stuff up. He tells me all the time that I better take this a little more seriously. He tells me we might have to take her to one of those exorcists to get the devil out of her. He then reminded me of the time he started to call one for me when he woke up one night and my head was spinning around. Luckily, he says, he just beat that thing up a little and I was just fine.

Harry swears sex cures me quickly, but I beg to differ. I think the devil is in him when I don't give him any.

"Anyway."

One night Beany told Harry she saw a ghost in her room.

Looking at him all sideways, I said, "Harry, now you know that girl didn't see any ghost. She just doesn't want to go to sleep."

Harry thought he was hosting *Unsolved Mysteries* and got right up from bed to investigate the situation. When he came back into the room, he was looking all concerned saying that Beany really did see something.

He only said that because he knew I was going to be scared.

"What did she see Harry?" I asked with chilled bumps on my arms.

"She said that she saw a little baby that had not been born yet because his soul was taken away before he was allowed to live," Harry answered.

"What did you tell her?"

"I told her if she ever sees him again to get an address so she can write," Harry said in a very serious voice. He then busted out in a loud spooky laugh.

27

I popped him behind his head wanting him to cut out that foolishness.

"Come on, Harry, this ain't funny."

"Really I told her if she sees him again to just say a prayer and it will go right away," Harry said.

Harry went on talking about it like it wasn't nothing. I kept telling him to shut up before he ends up sleeping on the couch, knowing all along I was not going to sleep by myself.

"Maybe if she has a gift like that, she could use it some day and make all of us rich," Harry said.

"Dang Harry! Now you're going to have my baby solving murders. Boy, go to sleep."

* * *

Harry always took time out for the children, and he's a very good husband. Whenever Alex or Beany had doctor's appointments, school events or anything I needed him to do for them, he would always be right there.

I remember when I was pregnant with Alex.

It was on a Saturday night.

Harry had all of his very ugly card-playing buddies over to the house. It had been a while since Harry had all of them over at once because the guys started breaking all the house rules.

The rules were simple:
No drinking hard liquid.
No smoking of any kind.
No loud profanity.
Absolutely no fighting.

All his rules were broken, so he decided to not have them over for a while. But this one particular time, I insisted that he have his friends over.

As soon as he found out I was pregnant with Alex, he went from good husband to super husband, never taking time out for himself. He didn't want me doing anything for myself, saying he wanted to make sure everything turned out fine. With all the extra care he was providing, he still didn't stop trying to get him some...every night. I think that was worst than anything he did for me when he called himself trying to help.

Alex was taking his sweet time coming. He was almost a week overdue. Some days Harry would take me riding to see if he could ride Alex out. He would ride across railroad tracks in Belcross, hoping that my water would break. The only thing that liked to have broken was my neck and his raggedy car.

A friend of mind, Nancy, told him if I would drink some cod liver oil, I would go into contractions, but I had taken so much of it when I was little and as nasty as that stuff was, I wasn't about to drink any of that mess.

After a while I was so tired of being pregnant, I took a teaspoon of it and went to bed. I was not any more good for Harry, that's why I insisted on him having that get-together.

After babying me to make sure I didn't need anything, Harry went to set up the table for the card game.

Knotts was the first to show up. I think Knotts had a little crush on me. Maybe if he got his teeth fixed, lost about 80 pounds, and combed his hair once in a while, he would make someone a pretty decent man.

Knotts came into the room.

"Hi Mrs. Harold," he said. "You sure look nice tonight, even if you are pregnant."

I guess that was supposed to be a compliment.

"Why thank you, Knotts," I said with a sweet smile, maybe teasing him a little.

"You can call me Donald," Knotts replied.

When he walked out of the room, I said in a low key "Thank you Donald. Now get the duck out because you 're quacking me up." I then started to laugh so hard I thought I felt a contraction. I then laughed every time I thought about.

Next, I heard a loud noise coming up in the yard. It sounded like it was going to blow up at any time. I didn't bother to get up and see who it was because I knew it was Lips. I didn't see him, but I could hear that loudmouth as he was turning up in the yard. As loud as his car was, his mouth was even louder.

As soon as he walked in the door, I yelled out, "Hi Lips."

"Tell yo' mama, 'Hi,'" Lips yelled back.

He knew I was picking on him, so he didn't feel like playing my little game. He wasn't that ugly. All he needed was a little face lift to fix those fat ass lips, a dentist to fix that big ass gap in his teeth, and someone to shave his body. Looking like big foot.

One time he smiled, and I saw a sign on one of his teeth saying next tooth fifty miles. I tried all these little harmless jokes on him, and they work every time.

Soon all the fellows were in place except Jr. Cefuss. I think he has found himself a girl friend. The sneaky thing about it is no one seems to know who, and Harry hasn't seen him in months. Other than my Harry, Jr. Cefuss was the closest to being normal out of the group.

Harry started with the house rules:

"Rule one: No cheating."

"Rule two: No loud cursing."

"Rule three: No smoking."

"And rule number four: No fighting. And if any of these rules are broken, I'm kicking somebody's ass."

They all started laughing. I think Harry was about tipsy by the time he gave out the rules, so it was going to be some crazy things happening before the night was over.

I was in the room talking with Teeny Baby on the phone. I was trying my best to get her to come over so we could listen in on Harry and the boys play cards. Sometimes you can find out a lot when you listen to them talk and carry on.

She said she could not stand any of Harry's friends. She said she doesn't want to have to shoot one of those ugly monsters. She says that Bucky looks like a moose with his bucked teeth and if a big game hunter ever spots him walking through the woods he would get shot on the spot. I told her they were funny to me and that I enjoy listening to them pick on each other.

"One of these days, one of them are going to try something when Harry's not around," Teeny Baby said.

"Girl they wouldn't harm a fly," I responded. I said to myself, with one good drink and a few dollars, she would be sleeping with any one of them.

Suddenly, I heard a loud noise and one of my glass's breaks.

Holding my stomach to brace myself as I got out of bed as fast as I could to see what was going on, telling

Teeny Baby I would call right back, with her yelling, "Don't mess around and lose that baby messing with those fools!"

When I walked into the room and there they were fighting. Bucky and Lips were going at it like dogs and cats. As a matter of fact, that's exactly what they look like.

I couldn't see what was really going on because Bucky's big ass teeth were in the way.

Harry made both get out of the house.

"If you two want to fight, do it outside," Harry said. They stopped fighting, walked outside, and started right back up again.

Harry was as sweet as they come but when he got around his friends, he was just as bad as they were. He stood at the door and watched as they tried to tear each other's heads off.

I guess I wasn't any better because all I did was stand there and laugh at the two of them. I have never seen so many lips and teeth flying in my life. Never have I seen Harry laugh so hard in my life either. Poor Lips was talking more than he was fighting. I think that he wanted someone to break it up, but Harry wasn't about to move.

Bucky finally got a good shot in and busted Lips mouth. Blood started flying everywhere, and big as his lips were, you know that it was about a bucket a minute. I yelled for Harry to go and break it up, but he was so busy yelling, trying to tell Lips how to get at least one good lick in before he gets knocked out, he could hardly hear me.

Harry looked over at me finally, seeing that I know longer found it funny. He asked Knotts to help him to break up the fight.

At first, I thought I was so excited that I peed on myself, but when those pains came a few seconds later, I realized that my water had just broke. Holding my stomach, and looking like I just saw an axe murderer, I screamed out for Harry. I guess me holding my stomach and having the look of death on my face scared them because Harry, Bucky, Knotts, and Lips all stopped in their tracks, Knotts holding Bucky and Harry with Lips.

"Damn girl, we're fighting, not shooting at each other," they all said at once. Suddenly, Harry caught on, asking me with that voice sounding like God talking to Moses at the burning brush, "Is it time?" He than looked on the doorsteps at the fluids leaking and said, "Yea, it's that time."

Harry was so excited he threw Lips to the ground and started bossing everyone around like he was some kind of general in the army. The first thing he did was told Bucky to go in the house and look in the bedroom by the bed, get the suitcase and put it in the trunk. "Lips," Harry said with a shit eating grin on his face, "You go clean that fat lip up a little because I want you to drive." Lips never say anything to Harry. To Lips, Harry can do no wrong, so he just stood there, and as loud as his mouth usually is, he was not saying anything. Knotts was standing there like he saw a ghost, so Harry told him to help clean up Bucky.

Each one of Harry's soldiers responded to all his commands, as Harry helped me out.

After Knotts helped Bucky get straight, he stood there like he saw a ghost for the second time. The only thing he kept asking was "Are you ok, Mrs. Harold?"

I kindly said, remembering that he had a little crush on me, "Hell, no! I'm having a baby."

Everyone was in the car in record time, everyone except Knotts.

We drove off with him standing in the same spot still looking at that ghost.

Harry got Bucky to drive so he could set in the back with me.

My contractions were about ten minutes apart, so I was starting to be in real pain.

With Bucky driving and Lips in the passenger seat, I knew I was in for a crazy ride. I knew I would be hurting one minute and laughing the next.

I couldn't help but ask Harry, "What was wrong with Knotts, and why was he just standing there like that?"

"As big as he is, he's about the scariest man I've ever saw," Bucky answered.

Harry said, "Yea, he doesn't have the stomach for any thing like this."

"His fat ass got the stomach for everything else, he was probably getting hungry," Lips said.

Everyone in the car started to giggle.

The next question I asked insured a good laugh.

"What were you two fools fighting about?" I asked, with a look of concern on my innocent looking face.

Bucky answered first with anger.

"I get tired of that fool always saying, 'your momma' whenever someone says something about him. He can't come back with a joke about you; no, he has to say, 'your mama' or something. I get sick of that. I done told his ugly ass about that one time."

"You know, Lips ain't doing nothing but playing," Harry explains to Bucky, laughing all the while. "He doesn't mean anything by it."

"He needs to control his mouth then," Bucky said.

Being that Lips could not stand me one bit, I decided to pour a little fuel onto the fire.

"Bucky," I said, "You know that Lips can't control those big ass lips of his. You are asking him to do the impossible."

"You better be glad I didn't have my knife," Lips told Bucky.

"You better be glad I didn't have my chap stick," Bucky replied.

Lips paused for a moment, trying to avoid another fight with Bucky. Instead of saying, "yo' mama," Lips said,

"If I had teeth like yours, I would be making money building river dams and porch decks, with your beaver looking ass."

I truly believe that I dilated about three more centimeters laughing at those two ugly fools.

Those two went at it all the way to the hospital, arguing like two little children, and poor Knotts, I wonder what time he finally left the house. I thought I was going to have a statue in the yard when I came back home.

Once I was in the labor room Harry was right there by my side. He had his little cap and gown on looking like a surgeon. He held my hand as he told me how much he loved me. At the same time, however, I was calling him every son-of- a-bitch in the book for putting me through all this pain. I didn't mean it, but I was just hurting so bad at the time. Harry was so scared that he agreed with everything I was saying.

Alex took his sweet little time but after about three hours he showed his face, coming out yelling like he had needles in his butt.

Harry stood there crying like he saw Jesus.

After Alex was born, I knew I wasn't going to have any more children, but two years two months later along came Beany with her bad self.

When I think back on it all I really miss them being babies because then they grow so fast. I guess that's why they say enjoy them while they're small because the next thing you'll know they will be grown and gone.

* * *

Alex was standing outside throwing rocks at the neighbors' dogs.

I ask him why?

Alex, looking just like me, said, "Every time I leave something on the porch, them dogs always taking it and carrying it a mile down the road. I'll find stuff two days later hidden somewhere in a ditch. One of these days I going to get me a BB gun and I'm going to shoot him right in the butt."

"If you put your things away instead of leaving them outside the dogs couldn't take your things," I said.

Alex is ten years old but looked much older for his age. I'm hoping he makes me some money one day. All I know is, Harry loves them so much, and they love him.

Me – I love my family.

CHAPTER 3
GHOST AND STUFF

Alex was at the free throw line and his team was down by one point. The score was twenty-three to twenty-four. Poor Alex was playing his little heart out, and my poor Harry was sweating like he was in the game playing.

"Mommy don't worry Alex is going to make both of them shots and he is going to win the game," Beany said to me with a sure and confident voice.

I asked Beany how she knew.

She just sat there with her fingers crossed and said, "I just know mom. I just know he will."

Alex bounced the ball about four or five times, concentrating on the rim the whole time. He spun the ball in his hands, positioned his hands on the ball with near perfect form, and then shot it up in the air with a high arch. Everyone in the gym watched as the ball went towards the rim. Nothing but net.

Beany and I jumped up, clapping our hands and giving each other high fives, and yelling to Alex.

"You go, boy!"

Right after the shot went in, the coach from the other team called for a time out. Alex and his teammates all gathered around Harry. Harry was the coach of the Boo-Cats, a Pee-Wee league team he and guys from the sawmill where he worked put together to give the children in the neighborhood something to do during their summer vacation. I think Harry's real motive was to make sure Alex was preparing for the NBA. He went so far as to buy the jerseys for the team. At first, I argued about him spending money on something that foolish, thinking that the least he could of did was make the other parents pay half. But Harry didn't respond to my argument, so I just let it go. After a while I soon figured out that Harry rarely bought anything for himself, while I spent mostly on myself, so I just let it ride.

After the time out, Alex went back to the free throw line. He repeated his ritual of bouncing the ball four of five times, spinning it in his hands, and concentrating on the rim.

Alex then shot the ball up into the air. The ball hit the rim spinning out of control.

Around and around the ball spun.

Inside the rim thousands of times, it seemed to spin.

The crowd all in "uuhh!" as it spun.

And the ball finally dropped in, winning the game, and breaking the "uuhhs" of disbelief into a loud cheer of relief. Even the parents cheering for the other team were clapping for Alex.

Beany looked at me.

"I told you, Mom," she said.

"You sure did, baby – you sure did," I said with a that grin on my face. You see, I could tell she was trying to start up that physic mess again. I tell you; she doesn't know who she is messing with. I was glad Alex won the game, but she kills me with her little grown self. I'm telling you; she better follow the light.

We left the bleachers, running down to congratulate Alex before he went to the locker room. I hugged Alex, making sure not to kiss him and embarrass him in front of his little Boo-Cats. I kissed my Harry, as he whispered in my ear, "Get it ready tonight." I was sure going to get it ready because he looked kind of sexy out there coaching.

After the game we headed to Alex's favorite restaurant.

Alex loved eating at Andy's. This was Alex's day, and Harry was going to make sure to oblige Alex's appetite with his favorite hero sandwich. Alex always went to Andy's and ordered the biggest hamburger he could with a side order of chili fries.

* * *

Alex is a bright kid. He makes good grades in school, and always tries to please his daddy. He tells his father he wants to be just like him when he grows up. Harry cherishes the fact that Alex loves to hang around him. Harry says, "That boy's going to make something out of himself one of these days." But then Harry goes on to say that Alex has one little problem: His mouth.

Harry says the boy asks too many questions sometimes. Harry said, "I know if you don't ask you may not find out, but that son of yours is ridiculous." I quickly reminded Harry he also asks a lot of questions. Just let me leave the house without telling him where I'm going, he would have a fit. I think it's not that Alex asks a lot of questions; it's the content of the questions.

Once Alex asked Harry, "Why did you and mommy pray so loud last night?"

Harry asked curiously, "What are you talking about Alex?"

Alex replied, "Last night, mom kept saying, 'Oh God! I'm coming,' and you yelled back, 'me too'. I thought you were leaving Beany and me to go to Heaven."

"As many questions as you ask, we were probably thinking about leaving," Harry told him.

I don't think Harry was ready to talk to Alex about the birds and the bees quite yet. Harry always took time out to explain most of Alex's questions, but when he didn't have a sure answer for one of Alex's questions, he would always tell Alex to wait, and we can find the answer together at the library. Alex loves to read, and his father often took him to the public library to use the computers. Sometimes, they would spend hours on the Internet if the library were not too busy.

There is an hour time limit on the computers, but if no one is on the list, the librarian, Miss Linda, lets them stay on it as long as they liked. Miss Linda is a very pretty lady young lady with long beautiful black hair. Harry says he thinks Alex has a little crush on her. I think it was just the other way around.

Harry and I had plans to get Alex and Beany a computer this Christmas.

Alex had one question that he asked Harry and me, and no matter how we answered him, he still managed to ask the same questions repeatedly.

"Why do I have to sleep in the same room as Beany?" Alex would ask with a frown on face.

"I get so sick of her talking about ghosts and stuff. Every night, she is talking to somebody or seeing something. Last night, she said she was talking to Great Grandma Amy, and Great Grandma Amy was telling her to tell me to be strong." Then Alex slipped and said loudly, "I get tired of that shit." I fully took the blame for him using that word because I used it a little too much at times, but I said nothing – only waiting for the verdict.

At first, Harry was listening like he was into everything that Alex was saying, but when Alex said the 'S' word, Harry forgot all about what Alex was telling him and popped Alex on the behind about four or five times, and, like God talking to Moses at the burning brush, told Alex to get to bed and think about what he just said.

I think that was the first and last time Alex got a spanking from Harry. Harry didn't like spanking the children. He says he got too many from his grandmother and he'd rather talk it out with his children. He also watched Oprah a lot, and he said he was looking at a show about spanking children and vowed not to spank Alex or Beany again. I knew it bothered Harry that he had spanked Alex because the very next day, he took Alex fishing. I'm sure he did this so it would give him and Alex a chance to discuss what happened the day before.

Me, on the other hand, I agree with Alex when it came to Beany seeing ghosts. I, too, was tired of hearing that shit. I think I'm the scariest person in the world.

I remember Ma Elsie sitting around the house when I was a little girl telling me how her mother, Grandma Amy, would see a black cat pass by her and she would turn around and go the other way. Or the time she told Lucky Jones she hoped one of his eyes popped out, and Lucky got into a car accident and one of his eyes was found on the steering wheel. The one story she told me that must have been true was the one about the young boys that threw a baseball and broke out her window. Ma Elsie said that Grandma Amy took the ball and put it high into a tree and said whoever takes that ball out of the tree will have bad luck. And to this day, that ball is still in the tree. Whenever I go to see Ma Elsie, I look at the tree and there it sits, all weathered and torn but still stuck in the tree. I never imagined I would have someone in my own home some thousand years later with ESPN or something. Most of the time, I tried not to put too much into what Beany would say, but on one particular Sunday, Beany and I were headed to see Ma Elsie.

Beany loves Ma Elsie because Mom would always talk to her about these things and ask her questions.

Beany was telling Mama she saw her Great Grandma Amy in her room one night.

"So, what did she say?" Ma Elsie asked Beany, as if she really believed her. "What did she have on?"

Beany told her that Grandma Amy had on a dress with different colored flowers in it and an old dirty white apron, and a scarf around her head with a straw hat on top of it.

Ma Elsie didn't say anything for a few minutes. She started to look for her spit cup. After finding it, she told Beany to go clean it out and come back so they could talk some more. I think Ma Elsie was getting Beany out of the room so she could gather her thoughts for a moment.

"Yes, Ma'am," Beany said and did as she was asked.

Alex always cried when he had to clean out the spit cup, and I would end up doing it for him. I always got stuck cleaning it when I was a little girl. Beany, on the other hand, didn't seem to mind. Maybe because Ma Elsie took time out to talk with her.

While Beany was cleaning out the cup, Mom asked me if I would look in her room and bring her some snuff. For a minute, I believed that she was getting me out of the room also.

When we all came back in the room, I handed Ma Elsie the snuff and Beany sat the cup by her rocker. Ma Elsie began to ask Beany another question.

"Beany", she said, "What did my mama say to you when you saw her?"

"She always telling me to tell Alex to be strong and, that's all she tells me," Beany answered.

I jumped up.

"That's enough of this stuff, Mom," I said. "You and Beany are starting to freak me out a little. Plus, you know, Beany ain't seeing no ghosts, yet you sit here and keep feeding her on. Mom, you know she must have seen some old pictures or something."

"Mom, I am telling the truth," Beany said.

"Brenna LaToya Harold, that is enough of that foolishness," I said. "Ma Elsie, you ought to be ashamed of yourself for carrying on like this with Beany. You're going to have the child in the crazy house."

I think what I was really saying was, "Stop it. Ya'll scaring the hell out of me."

So, when Alex said that he was sick of sharing a room with Beany, I kind of knew where he was coming from.

I would sometimes let Alex come and sleep with Harry and me if Harry was already asleep. If Harry awoke and found Alex in bed, he would pick Alex up and put him back in his own bed. Harry loved the children dearly but when it came to the bedroom, Harry put it like this: "I ain't having it."

* * *

After leaving the restaurant, we headed on to the house because Harry and Alex had another game to play tomorrow for the championship. Beany had already predicted that Alex's team was going to win, and, for one time, Alex did not seem to mind that she was using her powers on this one.

It was Saturday morning about 7:30 a.m. and Alex was already up. He was so excited about the game that he said that he couldn't sleep. He knocked on our bedroom door a few times and then came into the room to see if Harry was still going to work with him on his free throws. Harry got right out of bed. I believe he couldn't sleep either because he was eager to get started on this task.

They must have shot a thousand free throws because Harry finally told Alex that he did not want his arms to wear out. Harry went and sat on the steps and Alex went and sat down beside Harry. They then began talking about strategies for tonight's game. I remember Harry telling Alex that if he had an open shot, take it. Harry also told Alex, "Not to get upset if I yell a little – it's just that I might get a little excited since this is the championship game."

It was about that time.

Even I was a little anxious about the game.

We left about an hour earlier so the coach, Harry Harold, could get there and go over a few plays with the boys. The boys were only 9, 10, and 11 years old and probably never executed any of the plays Harry gave them, but I think it helped Harry's ego.

Before Harry could get out of the front door he got a call from the Johnson boys, Donnie, Maurice, and David. They did not have a ride to the game. For some reason their father nor mother was nowhere to be found.

There was all kind of rumors about what those boys were going through but folks mind their business in Camden as they spread the rumors. My Harry didn't hesitate to swing by to pick them up because they were the most athletic and gifted athletes, he had ever seen for their age. He also took a liking to them and would often ask me if he should confront their parents to see what was really going on with them.

When we got to the gym Beany, and I went and sat on the bleachers. Alex and Harry and the boys went into the locker room to change or whatever they do in there.

Soon it was tip off time. I heard Harry say, "Let's go, boys," and they took the court.

I never really liked ball games, but I loved to see Alex play because it was so funny to see the kids run around in circles. One time one of the boys shot the ball in the wrong goal. Being he made the shot, I clapped, cheered, and laughed until my side was hurting.

By the second half, Harry and the boys were losing so bad that I felt right sorry for them. The final score was 23 to 15, and Alex, poor soul, didn't make not one single point.

The Johnson boys David and Donnie scored all 15 points making them somewhat the heroes of the game... And somehow out of know where, their parents miraculously showed up to the game as it was ending. Stacy and James Earl stood as if to be mad that the boys was at the game...said nothing to Harry just got the boys and walked out of the gym, told them to get in the car and spun out the parking lot.

After the game, Harry told Alex how proud he was of him. I, too, gave him a big hug.

"Maybe next time, sport," I said. "Maybe next time."

"Beany," Alex said, "I thought you said we were going to win."

"I guess I was wrong," Beany replied.

Beany had that look on her face, as if she knew from the start, but it just proved to me she didn't do nothing but make that stuff up as she went along. Plus, for a minute, I thought I was going to have to start the papers on her.

"Well, do you feel like eating you hero sandwich tonight?" Harry asked Alex.

"I lost the game, not my stomach, Dad," Alex said. So, it was on to Andy's.

CHAPTER 4

FAMILY AND FRIENDS

The New Philadelphia Church of God and Christ was having Family and Friends Day. I had to get up a little earlier so I could cook for the church dinner we have after service and to get the children and Harry ready.

Family and Friends Day is a little fundraiser; we have, to raise money for the building fund. On Family and Friends Day, each member of the church collects money from family and friends. On the Fourth Sunday, you invite as many family members and friends as possible to the church.

For the last four years running, Ma Elsie always had the most family and friends to show up, but the Gregory's always raised the most money. And no matter what, it was a joyous day for the pastor. The most special thing for me on this day was that my husband, Harry, comes with the children and me to church. Harry says it is his one time of the year to shake the Devil off. I've even convinced my old buddy, Teeny Baby, to come out and join us. She said she was coming, but I don't know.

I hadn't talked to her in about a week and she was fussing me up something awful.

"Since you have your little family, you don't call me anymore," she complained.

And she was one hundred percent, absolutely right.

Harry and I were as close as you can get to having a perfect marriage. And I wasn't letting anyone step in and mess that up for us.

Not even Teeny Baby.

I think Teeny understands, plus she has settled down a lot since her breaking back days.

"Beatrice," Harry said, "you better put a move on it. It is almost 9:30 am."

For some reason, Harry gets all excited for Family and Friends Day. Maybe it's the one time of the year that he puts on his navy-blue suit and looks like a businessman. But before any of that happens, first it's . . .

"Baby, have you seen my blue socks?

Then, "should I wear my white shirt or my light blue one?"

And, last but not least, the old, "What tie should I wear?"

It's not like he has five or six.

"Red or blue? Just take your pick."

To tell the truth, I loved helping him get dressed. It kind of turns me on to see my man all decked out.

I had already got Alex and Beany dressed. They were sitting in the living room watching their dad – and me running round in circles trying to get him dressed.

Soon, we were all dressed, and it was time for Harry, the photographer, to mount the camera for the Fourth Sunday Family and Friends Day picture.

Once the timer was set, Harry would rush back over to the three of us. On the count of five Harry would say "Ready," and then we would all say, "Harry Harold."

One year, we all looked like we were whistling in the picture, so I think we only said, "Harry Hair," which leaves a beautiful smile on our face.

This was the fifth annual Family and Friends Day, and we got dressed in record time. In fact, we had time to spare.

Harry was putting the children in the car. Then phone rang. It was Teeny Baby. She couldn't get her car started and asked if we could stop by and pick her up. I knew Harry wasn't having that because every Sunday morning, Harry gets up early and washes his car. Afterwards, he puts a light coat of polish on it.

"It is to keep the paint from fading," he says, so I know he was not going to Teeny Baby's because she lived down a dirt road. Now, he would pick her up if she walked to the main road. And I knew Teeny Baby wasn't going to walk a mile and a half to the highway.

I told Harry that Teeny Baby needed a ride.

"Tell her to call a taxi!" yelled back Harry.

"Now, Harry, you know there ain't no taxis in Camden," I said.

"Tell her to call John D."

"John D. don't give rides on Sundays."

***

John D. was an elderly man that lived in Camden. He would fix your car or give you a ride anywhere you needed to go within 20 miles for a little feed or a promise to pay. If you didn't pay him and really needed a ride, he would be right there, and all you had to do was promise to pay him next time. But, if you called him on a Sunday, his grandchildren would be there to tell you, "John D.'s garage and taxi service is closed today," and hang right up. And if they ever found out you did not pay, they would come looking for you.

They once shot a man for getting a ride all the way to the airport in Norfolk, about 60 miles out, and the only thing he got paid was a jar of canned pickles, which John D. said was he fine with him.

49

"Follow me and I'll drive my car to pick her up," I said. I asked for him to wait on the side of the highway.

"That'll work," Harry said.

I told Teeny Baby I would be right there in two shakes of a horses tail and soon after we were on our way.

Harry and the children pulled off the side of the highway and waited. I turned on to the dirt path that leads to Teeny Baby's house. Harry also complained about how fast I drive on the dirt path, saying rocks will fly up and chip the paint on the car or crack the windshield. So, I made sure to drive slowly.

When I got there, Teeny was standing on the steps looking like a back up singer for Rick James. She had on a big red hat, a red dress with red stocking, and, to top it off, some red pumps with white lace on them.

"Teeny, come on now," I said when she got in the car. "You know it is too hot for all that red. You look like you just came from a Satan conference."

"I did," Teeny Baby said. "Me and your daddy went." We laughed and it was on from there.

"How's Alex and Beany?" Teeny asked.

"They are doing fine – just growing up too fast."

"That Alex is going to break some girl's heart one day," Teeny Baby said with a devilish look on her powdered face.

"I am glad you will be one hundred by the time he starts dating," I told her.

"One hundred is young these days, girl. And no matter what, I'll still look good," said Teeny.

Teeny Baby had no children, so she managed to keep her girlish figure and didn't mind flaunting it.

"Girl how's that Beany?" Teeny Baby said. "Is she still seeing things?"

"My baby don't be seeing nothing," I said. "She just has all you crazy people believing her."

"Yeah, well you didn't say that when you called me up sounding all frantic, telling me you think Beany was saying 'Red Rum,'" Teeny Baby said.

"Girl," I said, "I had just finished watching that crazy movie with Jack Nicholson, and she sounded like she was saying Red Rum to me, which is murder spelled backwards, which means that if she was saying that it was time for one of us to go."

Beany was just learning how to say her words and she was saying rest room. I think I needed some red rum that night.

Teeny Baby then went into that big red hat of hers and pulled out the dumbest question of the day.

"So, when was the last time you seen Alex's real father?"

"He's right ahead of us," I replied.

"You know who I am talking about."

"If he is the daddy, I am going to change Alex's name to Super Boy," I said. "Then to Aqua Man because I tied anything that came out of that man up in a condom and flushed it down the toilet."

Since Teeny Baby had to go there, I too went there. I asked her about Jr. Cefuss.

"Teeny Baby, I heard through the grapevine you and Jr. Cefuss had a little thing."

"No, you heard Jr. Cefuss had a little thing," Teeny Baby replied. "He was fine, I am not going to lie, but a cricket could swallow his little worm."

"Teeny Baby!" I said laughing. "You don't have a bit of sense. We better stop talking crazy and get ready for the Lord."

When we got to the church, the parking spaces all were taken, so we had to park in Cun Sophie's yard and hope she didn't shoot at the car. She didn't like for folks to park in her yard, although it did not have a lick of grass in it. Harry didn't take a chance. He rode around until he found a space.

We made our way inside the church. It was packed. If we would have come any later, we probably wouldn't have gotten inside. Teeny Baby whispered in my ear.

"Look who the guest speaker is."

I nodded, verifying that yes, I had seen.

The truth was I already knew the Reverend Tavone McKnight was the guest speaker, but I sure wasn't going to tell Teeny Baby and listen to hear her mouth all the way here.

Reverend McKnight's church was really growing, and the talk of the town was he's a very gifted preacher. I hadn't heard him preach yet because I left New Shady Creek and I joined Philadelphia years ago. I only joined Shady Creek because it was my husband's church. Since he never went, I came back to my mama's church.

After the choir had sung that song, you know the one they would sing before the preacher would preach, Rev. Andre Baxter introduced the guest speaker.

Rev. McKnight took the podium. He thanked Rev. Andre Baxter for inviting him and for the warm welcome. He then introduced his family.

"Before I start," said Rev. McKnight, "I would like to introduce the lovely people in my life. My beautiful wife, Trish McKnight; my son, Tavone Jr.; and my daughter, Candace."

Teeny Baby whispered again.

"She is not that beautiful with that ass fake hair." Teeny Baby just could not help herself.

Rev. McKnight went on to preach about the importance of family and the importance of having God in your family's daily plans.

Harry sat there in a trance, soaking in every word he was saying.

After Rev. McKnight was finished, it was time for the Rev. Dexter to announce who raised the most money and again, it was the Gregory's.

When family and friends were asked to stand up, Ma Elsie had the biggest group present, which was something Ma Elsie was proud of.

After service was over everyone went around getting reacquainted with loved ones, some they probably hadn't seen since last year this time.

The two preachers position themselves at the door so they could greet family and friends as they exited the door.

Rev. Andre Dexter and his family stood on the right side of the exit door; on the left stood Rev. Tavone McKnight and his family.

Harry was one of the first to exit the church. We were all walking holding hands like the lights were out and we had to hold on to Harry to find our way out.

Like always, Rev. Dexter told Harry how good it was to see him and how not to become a stranger.

"I'll be coming back soon," Harry replied as always.

"Thanks for coming out," Rev. Tavone McKnight said to Harry.

"No problem, man," Harry said. "I really enjoyed your speech . . . I mean sermon. I preach to my wife about family and who is in charge." Harry laughed, and then looked at me.

"Excuse me, Honey," Harry said. "Rev. McKnight, this is my wife, Beatrice; my son, Alex; and my daughter, Breanna." Rev. McKnight spoke and then introduced his family to us.

There was the eye contact between Rev. McKnight and me. Part of me wanted to slap the shit out of him and the other part of me wanted to slip him my phone number. I tried to stay cool so that Tavone wouldn't think I was studying him one bit and so Harry wouldn't notice my knees starting to knock a little.

We didn't say too much more because people were behind us, so we moved on out the doors.

Once outside, Teeny Baby pulled me away from Harry.

"Did you see the way Rev. Tavone McKnight was looking at you?" she asked. "It looked like Rev. McKnight saw God Almighty himself when Harry walked up so quickly to speak to him."

Teeny Baby swore that I had a nice-looking husband, but she said, "Rev Tavone McKnight was a god."

I thought she was going to go into that big red hat and pull out something else stupid, but instead she said, "I'll be over there with Ma Elsie so I can get me some of those chicken and dumplings she made." I called for Harry and the children to come so we could get in line to eat.

One thing about Family and Friends Day is, those church folk could surely cook, and I was not about to miss this dinner and have to go home to cook again.

After church, it was time to head for home. Harry wanted to stop the children by Tasty Freeze for ice cream and to pick up a movie from Belcross Fast Mart. Harry goes all out on Family and Friends Day and continues it with an extended family day at home where he shows a movie and makes popcorn.

I finally got up with Teeny Baby and we headed home.

On the way down the path to Teeny Baby's house, Teeny said,

"Beatrice, I know you and Harry have been through a lot, especially when ya'll first got married. But now I can say, I've never seen a happier marriage than I have seen with you guys. Girl, I wish I could find a man like Harry."

At first, I didn't know where she was headed with this, but she ended it beautifully.

When we got to her house, just for old times sake, she went pulling from the big red hat again.

"One day, you are going to tell me about Alex's daddy."

"Girl, you're the devil in a red dress," I shot back.

"Call me later if you need to talk about it," she called as I pulled off.

"Call me if that red ass dress sets the house on fire!" I yelled out the window.

CHAPTER 5
FIVE MIINUTES OUTSIDE OF GREENVILLE

We had been driving for about two hours headed for Goldsboro to visit Harry's twin sister, Harriet. She was stationed at Seymour Johnson Air Force Base and due to Harriet being his only sister, Harry tried to see her as often as possible.

We were about five miles outside of Greenville on US 13 when Harry was driving along listening to basketball, and the children and I were asleep, when a loud sound awakened us. Harry had passed out at the wheel. I grabbed the steering wheel to pull the car back on the road, then took my left leg and tried to move Harry's leg so I could mash on the brakes to stop the car.

I finally got the car to stop.

I jumped out and went over to the driver's side to see if I could help Harry. I told Alex to go around to the side of the road, take his shirt and try to flag down a car. Harry was still breathing but he was sweating profusely, and he kept coming in and out of consciousness. I was trying not to panic because of the children, but I couldn't help but cry uncontrollably.

There was not a lot of traffic on the highway but soon a big truck stopped and called 911 using his cell phone. After about fifteen minutes, an ambulance showed up. Harry was conscious but was not looking like the strong Harry I knew.

As the medics put Harry inside the ambulance, I told Alex and Beany to get in the car so we could follow the ambulance back to Greenville's Pitt Memorial Hospital. On the way to Pitt Memorial, Beany said, "Don't worry Mommy. Daddy is going to be just fine." For one time, I was hoping that she was right.

"Beany," Alex said, "I sure hope you know what you are talking about."

"I do," Beany said.

Following the ambulance, all I could think about was how much I loved Harry and how much Harry tried to make things right. Ever since the time Harry messed up, he spent everyday trying to prove he was sorry for he had done. I thought about the time when Alex was born and how Harry cried like a baby as he kept telling me how much he loved me and how he was going to make sure he would always be there for Alex.

"God," I prayed, "please don't let anything happen to my Harry," tears rolling down my face.

Once we were to the hospital, I parked the car, and the children and I rushed inside. I had to fill out some paperwork as they admitted Harry.

I waited in the waiting room for at least an hour before I could see Harry. While waiting, I called Harriet to let her know what happened, and she assured me that she was on her way. After an hour and thirty minutes of waiting, Dr. Warren finally came into the waiting room. I'm sure he could see that I wasn't taking this so well. With a soft and comforting voice, he reassured me Harry was going to be just fine. Dr. Warren said Harry just needed a little rest and to drink lots of fluids. He also told me Harry was a little dehydrated, but test results would show if there were any type of serious problem.

I asked Dr. Warren if I could see my husband. He smiled.

"Sure," he said. "You all can go and see him."

Alex, Beany, and I rushed to Harry's room. When we got to the room, I gently turned the doorknob, trying not to disturb Harry. I explained to Alex and Beany that they should be very quiet when entering the room.

When I turned the doorknob, all I could see was Harry's feet at the end of the bed, and all I could hear was the basketball game, the Hornets versus the Wizards. The curtain was pulled around and there was another family in the room, so Harry couldn't see us come in. We spoke to the family as we passed through.

When Harry saw that it was the children and me, he arose on the bed.

"When did they say I could leave?" he asked.

"They didn't," I told him, "But I'm sure you will have to spend at least 24 hours in here so they can monitor you."

"I'm a grown ass man and I can take care of my own self," Harry said.

"Right!" I said, "Just like you took care of us when your grown ass passed out behind the wheel."

Harry smiled.

"I guess you're right, Honey," he said. He paused.

"Beatrice, did you get in contact with Hiddy?"

"Yes," I responded. "She said she was on her way up here."

"Daddy, I know you was going to be alright," said Alex. "I think you was tired and me, mom and Beany didn't help any being that we were sleeping."

Beany cut in the conversation.

"Yeah, Daddy," she said. "You really scared me, but I knew you were going to be fine."

Harry just reached down to hug Alex and Beany.

Harry asked if I was going to stay with him or what. I told Harry that I was probably just going to get a hotel.

"That is a good idea," he said. "Then when Hiddy gets here, she can stay with the kids, and you can come back to stay with me." Harry had it all figured out without ever asking me if I wanted to spend my night here, even though I knew I wasn't going to leave my honey by himself. So really, the plan was good enough for me.

After about thirty minutes or so, a beautiful young nurse came in to check on Harry. She was shaped like she spent a lot of time in the gym.

"Hi", she said, "My name is Sheila Kite. I'll be your nurse for this shift. I'll be coming in here checking on you. If you need anything, just press this button and I or someone will be right here."

I looked at her with a crocodile smile.

"Thank you," I said. Harry also said thank you with a grin on his face. Once nurse Kite finished checking the IV bag, she told Harry, "Dinner will be here after a while." Harry said thank you, and she left the room. Harry turned to look at me.

"If you and the children are really tired, you don't have to come back tonight," he said.

"Harry! Don't play with me," I said. "I'd hate to hurt that young pretty nurse." Harry laughed.

"Baby, you know she ain't got nothing on you."

"Knock, knock, knock. It's Hiddy," Harriet said.

The children ran to her, happy to see her.

Hiddy always sends the children things from the different places she goes with the military. She especially loves Beany.   She calls Beany her little fortune baby. She swears Beany gives her good luck.

I decided to let Hiddy, and Harry catch up on some lost time, so the kids and I left to get us a hotel for the night. Hiddy agreed to stay with the children while I stayed at the hospital with Harry.

* * *

On the way to the hotel, I started reminiscing about the time Harry and I first met. It was a hot summer day, and I was headed back to Camden from Elizabeth City State, when a turtle ran across the road. Well, it looked like it was running. Maybe because it was so hot the pavement probably was burning its feet.

Me being the animal rights activist I am, I tried to dodge so I wouldn't hit the poor thing. I missed the turtle and ran dead into the ditch.

Sudie May Collons lived up the road less than a mile, so I went there to call a tow truck, and walked back to my car to wait.

What happened next change the course of my life forever.

A tall sweaty god stepped out of that truck. As he walked towards the car, he seemed to be moving in slow motion, each muscle ripping in that wife beater Tee shirt as he took each step.

"That's just my baby's daddy," I said to myself.

When he began to talk, I think that was the first time I heard God talking to Moses with the burning bush voice.

"How did this happen, Ms. Lady?" he asked.

After I told him the story about the turtle running across the road, he laughed and said, "That's a first. A running turtle, ya say?"

"Yes, a running turtle," I said with a smile as big as Texas on my face.

After pulling my car out of the ditch, he noticed that my tire was flat and offered to fix it for me, no charge.

He gave me a business card and told me to call if I needed fixing. I called and, needless to say, I started to break down almost everyday.

Harry was five older than me and said that he remembered me as a little girl. He said if he had known that I was going to grow up to be this fine, he would have given me candy every time he saw me until I come of age.

* * *

Once we got to the hotel, we unpacked. I decided since the children had been through so much, we all needed a little break. I told the children we could go to Wendy's for dinner and then catch a movie before I headed back to see their dad. Beany was glad to have her Aunt Hiddy to stay with because Hiddy let them stay up late and eat a bunch of junk food. Alex asked if he could come back to the hospital with me to see Harry.

"I rather be with you and daddy," he said.

"Alex, your dad needs lots of rest right now, and he may need my help with something," I told him. "Plus, there is no where for you to sleep."

"Well, okay," he replied, but I could tell he was disappointed, although I knew he understood.

It was about 5:30 p.m. when we headed back to the hospital to see Harry. I had called him at least five times while we were out and couldn't wait to get back to see him. When I walked back in the room, Harry and Harriet were both asleep.

"Hiddy," I softly said.

"I am just resting my eyes," she replied.

Hiddy sat around for an hour or two talking about old times, and then it was time to take the children on back to the motel. Hiddy left with the children, assuring Harry and me the children were in good hands. She winked at the kids and smiled.

Harry and I talked for a while. He told me while I was out, the nurse said that he would be leaving tomorrow and that all the tests turned out to be fine. Harry decided we would head back tomorrow.

I decided I would drive.

CHAPTER 6
LITTLE SHORT COMINGS

It was the last game of the season, the big dance, the NCAA Championship game. Even I enjoy watching this one game. My favorite team didn't make it to the dance this year, but I know they will be back. The UNC Tar Heels have a tradition of winning, so I know they'll come back with a vengeance.

Harry, on the other hand, was a Duke fan, and he was hurt when they got knocked off by Indiana. Harry picked Maryland to win it all after Duke got beat. So, I had to go with Indiana.

This was a very busy day.

My job was to buy the beer and the food. Since I didn't drink, I would usually buy wine coolers for Teeny Baby and me. Then, I had to take Beany and Alex to Ma Elsie's house. She looked forward to them coming and would make them cookies and pop popcorn and put her old cassette player in the living room so she could dance and play with the children. Harry's job was to turn the garage into a sports bar. He called on his friends to help, but the only one he could count on being there was his friend Bucky.

I left Alex and Beany with Harry. I stopped by and picked up Teeny Baby and we were on our way. The one store we usually stopped by for fun had some meaning. Wal-Mart, just like the commercial says. We could get the beer, the ribs, and chips without leaving to go somewhere else to look for our outfits. Yes – we had to have something to wear, especially Teeny Baby.

She always looks for a husband. She does not admit it, but I see it in her eyes whenever I talk about Harry or the children. She didn't have that big red hat

63

on today, but I knew she was reaching in her purse for something besides lipstick. What she pulled out next surprised me. Teeny Baby asked what I thought about her and Cefuss.

"What do you mean?" I asked.

"You know," Teeny Baby said. "Do you think he is a nice man?"

"Teeny Baby, it's not what I think. It's how you feel that counts."

"You know I tell you almost everything and, girl, I'm telling you, I'm falling for him like a fat lady off the Golden Gate Bridge," she said. "I mean he's always nice and he gives me whatever I ask for. And the sex. He tries to make up for his little, short comings, if you know what I mean".

"Girl, you're never going to find out if you don't try," I said.

"I've been trying for quite some time, so I guess you're right," she said.

I too had to go in my purse, so I pulled out something I've been wanting to know for quite some time.

"Teeny baby, that night I asked you to come over and to hang out with me when I was pregnant with Alex, and the boys had that card game going, were you seeing Jr. Cefuss then?"

"Girl, that's been so long ago. I don't..." Teeny started. Then she paused for a moment.

"Hell, yeah!" she said. "I let him try to break my back, but he couldn't even crack it. That's why I had to let him alone, but he kept being persistent over the years. That's why I asked you. You are the relations expert, you, and that fine Harry."

"Girl," I said, "you know Harry and I have been through our ups and downs."

"But you two manage to make it work," said Teeny Baby.

"Yes, and it took a lot of work," I said.

We really enjoyed ourselves, shopping and talking about some of everything.

After dropping off Teeny Baby, I headed for home. When I pulled up in the yard, there they were in no curtain order: Harry, Bucky, Jr. Cefuss, Lips, Knots, Alex, and even my little baby, Beany, in the garage turning it into Harry's sports lounge. Harry had built a big wooden box to put the big screen TV on when he brings it out of the living room. Harry also sets his favorite chair out in the garage. Everything that is usually in the garage is placed back in the storage shed.

Harry came over to help get the bags out of the car.

"I'm sure glad all the guys came over to help out," Harry said to me.

I think the guys knew if they didn't help, Harry would try to do it all himself, and they knew about what happened to Harry when we were on our trip to Goldsboro.

After the garage was set up, all the guys left. Jr. Cefuss called me to the car. I already knew what he wanted.

"Let me ask you a question and don't lie," he said. "Does Teeny Baby ever talk about her and me?"

"Why do you ask me that?"

"I know she told you that I got a thing for her," he said.

"Oh, yeah," I said, acting like I didn't know.

"Beatrice, stop playing. You know we've been seeing each other."

"What's the point?" I said Sarcastically. "What do you want to know?"

"Okay," Jr. Cefuss said, "here's the point. I'm going to ask her to marry me tonight at the game. What do you think about that?"

"I think that's beautiful, Jr. I think you two make a wonderful couple. Do you already have the ring?"

"What do you think? Yeah, I've got the ring," Jr. Cefuss said.

"Does Harry know about this?" I asked.

"No, but he will tonight," said Jr. Cefuss.

Lord, Harry is going to have a fit when he finds out that Teeny Baby and Jr. Cefuss are an item. Harry swears that Teeny Baby ain't right. Harry says Teeny Baby was just a little too fast for her own good. He wonders what I see in her. He has never forbidden me from seeing her. Even if he did, it wouldn't matter. I looked at it like this: at least I know how she is. It's the ones that smile in your face that I don't trust.

It was getting late, and I promised Ma Elsie that I would have the children over to the house by 5:30. I gathered their clothing and asked Harry if he needed anything while I was out. Surprisingly, Harry said, "Stop by the ABC store and get a half a gallon of Hennessey."

Alex and Beany went over to Harry and gave him a big hug. Alex didn't want to go, but Harry didn't allow Alex to stay because of the drinking that would take place. He would always tell Alex, "When you turn twelve, it will just be you, me, Mom and Beany at Harry's Sports Bar and we'll only drink Kool-Aid". And Alex was looking forward to that day.

Beany told Harry to give her one more hug and one more kiss. Harry was like, "Sure, Baby Girl. Anything for my Beany."

Beany whispered something in Harry's ear. I could not hear what she said.

"Oh, really!" Harry replied. "Well, I better give you and Alex one more hug." He reached down and hugged Beany once more.

"I think I had enough hugs for one day," Alex said. Harry placed the palm of his hand on top of Alex's head.

"Alright, little man. We straight," Harry said.

The children and I got in the car and headed to Ma Elsie's house. I notice Harry was just standing there staring as we drove off. I started to wonder what Beany had said to him. Both Alex and Beany were looking so sad. I had to say something.

"Cheer up, kids," I said. "Ma Elsie don't want to see you two with those long faces." Alex usually has a distant look on his face, but Beany usually can't wait to get to Ma Elsie's.

"Beany," I said, "you don't want to go to Ma Elsie's house? You are usually excited."

"Yes, I'm just going to miss Daddy," Beany said.

"You're not going to miss me?"

"Yes, I am going to miss you, too mama," Beany said.

When we turned in the driveway, Ma Elsie was sitting on the porch waiting for us. Once Beany saw Ma Elsie, she was all smiles. She hardly could wait for me to put the car in park before she jumped out the car and ran up to Ma Elsie.

"Hey, Grandma Elsie," Beany said. "What are we going to be doing tonight?"

"We got some good movies to watch, and I made your favorite cookies," Ma Elsie said.

"Do you have the popcorn, too?" Beany asked.

"Yes," said Ma Elsie.

Alex took his time getting out. He helped get all the bags from the car and walked up to the porch, trying not to look up so he wouldn't have to speak.

"Boy, you better say 'hi' to your grandmother," I said.

Alex looked up with his bottom lip touching the porch.

"Hi, Ma Elsie."

"Hi, sweetheart" Ma Elsie said.

I told Alex he'd better straighten up.

"Leave him alone," Ma Elsie said. "He'll be just fine." About five seconds later, Alex ran to the porch.

"Wow! Thanks Ma Elsie."

"What?"

"Grandma got me a play station with NBA 2002," Alex said.

"Mom, you know that didn't make no sense," I said.

"You and that tight butt Harry ain't gonna buy nothing," Ma Elsie snorted.

Alex and Beany went inside and started playing with the games. Ma Elsie and I sat on the porch for a while, and then it was time for me to go. I went to tell Alex and Beany good-bye, but they were so busy playing that they barely raised their hands to wave.

Beany yelled out, "Tell Daddy I love him", and Alex said, "Me, too."

"What about me?" I asked.

And simultaneously, they said, "We love you, too, Mom."

It was about seven o'clock when I got back to the house. I had to get ready quick because I knew that guests would be showing up soon. The game started at 8:30. All Harry's friends had gone home to get dressed. I didn't see Harry when I drove up, so I knew he was in the shed and he knows I was not about to go back there.

Once, I was back there getting the lawnmower out and I saw a snake. I haven't been back there since. Harry goes out in there and spends hours at a time listening to old 45 records or his eight-track tape player. He says the shed is the one place he can go and don't have to worry about being bothered. The children, bless their hearts, won't step near the shed. Harry, after killing the snake, showed it to the children and told them the snakes only come out when someone comes in here that doesn't belong.

Jr. Cefuss was the first to show up. Normally, it would have been Bucky, but Jr. Cefuss had all the motive in the world to get here first because he knew Teeny Baby would be here early.

He came in and asked where Harry was. I was in the room getting dressed, so I yelled.

"He's out in the back in the shed."

"It figures," Jr. Cefuss said.

Harry came in the house and got ready while Jr. Cefuss started cooking on the grill. After I got dressed, I went out to see if there was anything I could do to help. Harry had everything done, so I just waited on Teeny Baby, and, like clockwork, she was right on time. She looked decent for a change. Her jeans were a little tight and her shirt was a little revealing, but she looked good. Poor Jr. Cefuss acted like he just saw the playboy centerfold or Jet magazine beauty of the week. He was looking at Teeny Baby so hard that he almost burned the ribs.

Teeny Baby and I were talking about how we were going to get the party started. First, we strategically positioned ourselves so we could greet and critique the guests after we had a wine cooler to get us in the mood.

Bucky and Lips were also among the first to show up. "Bucky, Lips, glad you could make it," said Teeny Baby.

"Wish you hadn't," said Lips.

"Now you don't mean that, Lips. You haven't seen a woman this fine since you saw me last time," said Teeny Baby.

"He ain't seen much with his eye hiding behind those big ass lips," I said.

"Of course," Lips said. "Yo mama." Bucky reminded him about that "Yo mama" stuff.

"She ought to watch her mouth, always taking up for that ugly Teeny Baby," Lips said.

After they went over to get a drink, they went outside and stood around with Jr. Cefuss at the barbeque pit. Harry came out of the room with a smirk on his face, telling Teeny Baby and me not to mess around and cause Lips to go off, saying he heard Lips was on that stuff.

"Did Bucky bring the one loaf of bread again this year?" Harry asked.

"No, he brought hamburger rolls this year," I said.

Bucky always felt like he had to bring something. We're just waiting for him to bring some meat or beer, or something he eats or drinks.

"Who in the hell invited her," said Teeny Baby.

"Who are you talking about?" I asked.

"Look."

"Dang! Who in the hell did invite her?"

It was the most lying, nosiest, gossip of the town – not to leave out fake ass, female in town. She walked up.

"Hi, ya'll."

"Hey, girl," Teeny Baby and I said with smirks on our faces.

"What brings you out here, Lucy Gay?" said Teeny Baby, like it was her party.

"Bucky told me that he was having something over here at the Harold's, so I decided to come out."

I smiled (shit eating grin of course), and said, "Well, glad you decided to come."

"Where is Bucky?" said Lucy Gay.

"He's in the garage with the rest of the guys," said Teeny Baby.

Lucy turned and walked out, knowing she was so wrong for even showing her face.

"Beatrice is it me or did Bucky invite her so she could help him eat those hamburger buns," said Teeny Baby.

"Maybe he wants her to eat his Bucky burger," I said, and with that it was on.

A few more guests arrived, and we went to mingle with them. The game stared soon after and everyone was glued to the big screen. Teeny Baby and I were so busy talking about folks that we didn't even keep up with the game. We, like always, ended up being waitresses for the guests, fixing drinks, cooking the food, and serving it hot off the grill. By half time, most of the food was gone except for Bucky's hamburger buns, and I was waiting to see if him or his guest were going to eat those.

Lips and Bucky rode together to the party, but you couldn't tell because they were both drinking like they were going to start attending those AA meetings first thing Monday morning. Teeny Baby called me over to the side.

"Look at Lips," she said. "I think he is trying to hit on Lucy Gay."

Lips was fixing her drinks and telling her how good she looked. Bucky was getting a little jealous and the alcohol wasn't helping any. Teeny Baby was trying to get something started, so she walked over to Bucky.

"Didn't you invite Lucy Gay over to the party?" she asked.

"Yeah," Bucky replied.

"Why are you letting Lips take your woman?" Teeny Baby said.

"I really want you," Bucky said.

Teeny Baby pretended that she didn't hear him and said, "Boy, go get your woman."

Bucky went over where Lips and Lucy Gay were talking.

71

"You're so fine, I would drink your bath water," Lips told Lucy Gay as Bucky walked up.

"As big as your lips are, you should be using those soup coolers to cool the bath water," Bucky said to Lips.

Lucy Gay along with everyone in Harry's Sports Bar and Grill began to laugh.

"Your fat ass mama got big lips," Lips replied, and with that the two got into a heated confrontation.

Harry stepped in and told the two if they wanted to fight, they needed to take their drunken as behinds home. Lips, avoiding the situation, just walked back to his chair, and waited for the second half of the game. Knotts said that he wanted to make a toast, so everyone reached for a glass, mug, or whatever they had near their hands at the time.

"Here's to my good friend Harry for having another slamming party at Harry's Sports Bar and Grill," Knotts said.

Everyone said, "Cheers," and took a sip of whatever they were drinking.

Jr. Cefuss reached into his pocked as he called Teeny Baby over to him. Everyone got quiet.

"Teeny Baby," Jr. Cefuss said.

"Stop!" Teeny Baby said. "If you're going to ask me, call me by my first name."

I knew right then she was going to say yes because she despises her real name.

"Let me try this again," Jr. Cefuss said. "Ms. Ella May Sarah Cobb, will you marry me?"

"Yes, I will marry Mr. Cleophus Joe Taylor, Jr.," Teeny Baby said.

Everyone began to clap and cheer.

"With that note, I'm going to get the last of the food off the grill," Harry said. Harry was happy that one of his friends was getting married, even if it was to my friend Teeny Baby.

The game started back, and everyone was settling down. Then, we heard a loud noise outside. Knotts got up to see what it was. At the same time, the phone rang, so I went to answer the phone. It was Ma Elsie.

"Is everything alright?" she asked.

"As far as I know it is."

Teeny Baby then yelled for me to come outside.

"Just a minute," I said.

"You better come now!" said Bucky.

"Ma Elsie, I'll call you back." I hung up the phone and ran outside to see what the big fuss was all about. The first thing I thought was those two fools, Bucky, and Lips, had all all but killed each other in one of their usual drunken fights. Before I could get outside, Jr. Cefuss came over.

"I don't think you need to see this," he said.

"See what, Jr. Cefuss," I said sarcastically.

"Harry...."

Before he could finish, I was like, "Harry!" and ran over to the grill and there he was lying on the ground. The grill was turned over on the patio, and everyone was trying to help. All I could do was cry out, "No, God, please no, not my Harry!"

I couldn't move, I couldn't even think. I couldn't remember who I was at this moment. Suddenly, none of this seemed real. There my life was, lying lifeless, slipping away, and there was not one thing I could do but cry.

They tried to save my Harry, but he was gone.

The police came and Officer Hutton asked me some questions. I guess they wondered because of the way Harry had fell over the grill, and then pulled it on top of him. She was very polite, and I tried to answer as best I could.

The phone rang. It was Ma Elsie again. She asked me was everything okay. I told her what happened to Harry.

"Beany was yelling and crying for Harry and when I asked her what was wrong, she said Harry left to be with Grandma Amy," Ma Elsie said. "She was crying so hard I was going to ask if she could speak to him over the phone." She paused.

"I am so sorry, baby. Are you okay?" said Ma Elsie.

"Yes, Ma, I'll be just fine. I'm going to have to leave it in the hands of the Lord," I said. "How is Beany now? What is she doing?" I asked.

"She is doing fine. She's sleep now."

"Where is Alex?" I asked.

"He is still playing the game," said Ma Elsie.

"Well, don't tell them anything. I'll be over there later to spend the night once I clean this mess up," I said.

"Beatrice, don't you worry," Ma Elsie said. "You're going to be alright."

"I know, Mama," I said.

The game was long over. All, the guests were gone except Teeny Baby, Jr. Cefuss, Bucky, Lips, and Knots.

Lucy Gay was probably out calling everyone she could think of right now. You see, that's her job as the town gossip collector.

Teeny Baby and the rest of the gang had cleaned up everything and asked if there was anything else they could do to help. I told them no and thanks for being there for me. They all eased out with soft good-byes and a confirmation that they will, for sure, see me tomorrow to help tear down Harry's Bar and Grill for next year.

Teeny Baby asked what I was going to do. I told her I was going over to Ma Elsie's house to be with the children. Teeny Baby insisted that she was going to drive me over to Ma's house, so we packed my stuff.

Since Harry was pronounced dead on arrival, there wasn't any need for me to hang around the hospital. All I wanted to know was what happened to him. Why did he just die like that?

Harry never complained of chest or head pain, or anything. Other than the one time he passed out when he was driving, he never had any problems. By the time we got to Ma Elsie's house, it was a little after 3 a.m. Ma Elsie was sitting waiting for me. She said she just couldn't see Harry dying at such a young age. Harry was five years older than me, but he looked much younger, and he was in such good shape.

Ma Elsie never talked much about Daddy. She says that only life is important and when she thinks about Daddy, she tends to question her own mortality.

This morning, for some reason, maybe out of comfort, she talked about my daddy.

"Your daddy," Ma Elsie said, "died when you were only three months old. I had to raise you all by myself. He was a very strong, proud man, just like your Harry, and often Harry reminded me of him. I never told you how he died. It was so painful to talk about. I want you to hear this from me."

"Charlie Daniel Barker," she said, shaking her head, and then smiling. "Woo, that fine Charlie Barker. You know I found him dead in the potato field under the plow. Those sharp heavy blades had almost cut him in half. He fell backwards off the tractor. Don't think Ma Elsie can't feel your pain because I have been there. Every time I see you, I see him, and you have been my strength and inspiration. Now you have Alex and Beany for strength, and always remember God has got a plan."

Ma Elsie and I talked until finally I fell to sleep in her arms like a little baby.

CHAPTER 7
THE SHIP 'ENTERPRISE'

I was sitting in my favorite spot behind the house, ducking the sun's last attempt to keep darkness at bay. My mind was slipping in and out of reality. I've come to grips with the passing of my husband, but the ghost of hope paralyzes me, and I dream of us being together once more. Harry, in so many ways, helped me to define who I am and what I stand for as a woman. He showed me that I could be strong yet loving, and most of all, he taught me the meaning of forgiveness.

It has been three weeks since they placed Harry into that dark hole at New Shady Creek Baptist Church cemetery. For some reason, I just can't see my husband going into the ground, and, for some reason, it just doesn't seem right. You see, at one time, it was where dead people go. Now it's where people that once lived are. Maybe that's just like me, giving life to a cemetery. If Harry has anything to do with it, there will be a sports bar somewhere down there, and he will be watching TV.

The funeral was so ironic.

Although Harry never went to New Shady Creek, it was the church he belonged to and that's where most of his family belonged. Harry's mother and father died in a car accident when Harry was three, so he was raised by his grandmother. His grandmother died when Harry was eighteen, so it's been he and his sister Hiddy pretty much since.

Reverend Tavone McKnight was preaching at my husband's funeral. Now, imagine how I must have felt listening to someone I had an affair with, not only constantly staring me in my face, but also sending my husband to his grave at the same time.

I did some crying that day – hell, that week.

It seems every time I sit back here in my favorite spot, I can just place all things in their right place and understand how God has blessed me. Teeny Baby hasn't called me in a couple of days. I guess she's trying to give me space, which I so much need.

It was time for Alex's pee-wee league baseball tryouts. I knew nothing about baseball, but I would go out in the back yard to play catch with him. He would tell me that he wished his daddy was here to hit the ball so he could practice catching the high in the air ones or the hit on the ground ones. I tried that, but I knew I wasn't doing anything to help. Maybe me just being there helped. I did manage to hit some on the ground by my feet ones though.

Beany, I think, didn't fully understand what was going on. Whenever she talked about Harry, she would talk as if he was right there in the house. Sometimes, I would overhear her talking, like she was talking to him.

Ma Elsie told me that the night Harry died, Beany had told Harry that Grandma Amy said it was time for him to come home and that he was leaving that night. When I think about it, I do remember Beany whispering in Harry's ears and saying something as Harry said to Beany, "I better give you another hug." Yes, I really do remember that. I also remember Beany being so sad and that she kept saying that she was going to miss Harry.

For once, I wanted Beany to tell me Harry was around. I wanted to know if he says "hi" or asks about me. I never really believed that kind of stuff, but I wanted to, now more than ever.

It was time to take Alex to baseball tryouts.

Beany didn't want to go to the tryouts. She didn't like the boys and mosquitoes and gnats flying around, so I took her over to Ma Elsie's house. She spends quite a bit of time with Ma Elsie since Harry passed and Mama was loving every moment of it.

Alex and I headed out to Knobbs Creek Ball Park for first tryouts. On the way, I told Alex not to forget everything I showed him today.

"Mom," Alex said, "if I forget everything you showed me, I will have a better chance of making the team." I smiled because all I was really trying to do was be there for him. I didn't really worry about Alex making the team because being from a small place, not that many were trying out. Alex was a little upset because girls could even go out for the team this year.

When we arrived, Alex saw the Johnson brothers and barely waited for the car to come to a complete stop before he grabbed his glove, jumped out of the car, and ran over to be with his friends.

Parents weren't allowed on the field, so I parked the car and walked over to the bleachers to sit and spectate. I heard a faded voice in the distance call out.

"Hey! Mrs. Harold."

I looked around and it was Reverend McKnight walking toward the bleachers. I was looking around for the rest of the gang, but he was by himself.

As he walked toward the bleachers, I didn't exactly know how to act or why he was even walking this way. I know he didn't follow me out here, or did he? The closer he came, the more paranoid I was getting. He came right up.

"How are you doing, Mrs. Harold?" he asked.

I hardly answered before asking him, "What brings you out here?"

"T.P.," he answered.

"Who?"

"T.P., my son. Tavone Jr. We call him T.P. He hates being called Jr. I also stopped by and picked up the Donnie David and Maurice," Tavone replied.

"The Johnson boy, Beatrice said with a little disbelief in her voice. That crazy husband and wife team don't let anyone close to them and I heard some crazy things were going on around there. Hey, but it ain't none of my business."

"Yea I guess," Tavone said.

"So, how have you been doing, Mrs. Harold?"

"Please, just call me Beatrice," I said, "and I have been doing fine."

I put up my guards like Roy Jones Jr. himself just invited me to a fist fight and I wasn't about to let my guards down to get sucker punched by a country ass preacher.

"Look, I'm not here to say anything out of the way. I just wanted you to know if you ever needed someone to talk to, I'm always available," said Reverend McKnight.

I felt a little bad for being so hard on Tavone, so I immediately apologized for being so defensive.

Tavone just made promises that he didn't keep. He was such a smooth talker. The times I was with him I was in my most vulnerable state anyway. First, it was Harry's cheating that caught me off guard. The second time was when Harry and Alex went to spend a week with his sister. I promised God and myself I would never be caught with him touching me again, dead, or alive.

I know now that Harry's gone, and I couldn't be with anyone, or want anyone, to so much as touch me. In a way, I hated Tavone and what he stood for as a man. I decided since he wanted to talk, I was going to talk but it wasn't going to be what he thinks it's going to be about.

The only thing I had next to me was Alex's gym bag, so I reached in the bag and pulled out a question that I knew was going to knock his socks off.

"Reverend, how did you feel preaching at my husband's funeral knowing you had slept with his wife?"

"Come on now, Beatrice," Tavone said. "What kind of question is that?"

"A question I want an answer to kind of question."

"Okay, I'll tell you how I felt," he said. "I felt like God was trying to tell me something."

"Yeah, like you're going to hell," I said.

"Come on now, Beatrice. You asked me, and I'm trying to tell you what I felt," said Tavone.

"I'm sorry. Go ahead."

Tavone took one of those handkerchiefs that preachers are known in the South to carry around in their pockets and wiped off his face.

"It seemed like the whole church was looking at me as if they were saying how could he do this," he said. "I felt like they all knew for a fact that you and I had something going on."

"You know that Lucy Gay is a member of your congregation, and she's worse than any tabloid magazine you could ever read," I said.

"Even Trish asked me why I was so nervous, and I told her I wasn't nervous, that I just felt a little ill that day," Tavone explained. "And then, it was your little girl."

"What about my little girl?" I asked.

"She was staring me right dead in my face the whole time I was preaching. Even when I focused on something and looked back at her, there she was looking dead at me with not one tear in her eyes," explained Tavone.

"Well…You know she's been saying some strange things in her little life span. She tells my Mama she sees Harry all the time and that she talks with her Great Grandma Amy. Some of the time, she has even guessed little stuff like if Alex was going to win a game or what her Great Grandma Amy was wearing when she died. As a matter of fact, she told Ma Elsie that Harry was going home to be with Grandma Amy the night that he died. From what Ma Elsie says, she even mentioned it to Harry before she left to stay with her that night."

"Tavone," I asked, "what do you think about that kind of behavior?" At first, Tavone went to his Bible for the answer, quoting sometimes from Matthew, Chapter 17, which he says speaks of reincarnation. Tavone was a gifted preacher. He mixed his philosophies with his twisted interpretation of the Bible so that it would fit any problem-solving life equation. In other words, he tried to tell you what he thought you wanted to hear.

"You can take a gift, like – what's her name?" Tavone said.

"Beany," I said.

"Like Beany's said Tavone and compare it only to a child that plays Mozart, or a violin, like…. It's a gift from God, and just look at it like that, a gift."

T.P. and Alex came over to where Reverend McKnight and I were sitting.

"Dad," T.P. said, "How's my catching?"

"Yeah, Mom, how's mine?" asked Alex.

"Great!" we both replied. "You boys are going to be the best on the team."

They were on a water break, so they ran back over with the rest of the boys.

"Did you even see them play?" Tavone asked.

"No," I said, and Tavone replied, "I missed it, too."

"We are starting with the lying again," I said. "And it started with you lying first."

"Anyway," Tavone said, "Now about your little girl. I knew she was special the way she looked at me that day."

"Beany, I know, has some kind of gift, but she still goes off the deep end sometimes. When she talks about seeing dead people or whatever, she will say that she sees a girl called Wendy with another child that has not been born yet, is how she puts it," I said.

Tavone looked as if he himself had seen a ghost.

I got on the intercom of the spaceship "Enterprise" and asked Scottie was it okay if I beamed Tavone back to earth.

"Mom, can I spend the night with T.P.?" said Alex.

"Maybe some other time, if it's okay with Reverend McKnight and Mrs. McKnight," I said.

"Sure, you can stay over some time," Tavone said.

"Hey, cool," Alex replied. "T.P. and I can practice together sometime."

"Tavone, thanks for listening and sorry for being so cold," I said.

"Make sure that you come out to New Shady Creek sometimes," Reverend McKnight said.

"I'll make that a promise," I said.

On the way home, Alex said, "There is something about Reverend McKnight. He is cool; he's not like Reverend Baxter. He acts like he knows where kids are coming from."

"Yeah? Well, he's an okay guy," I said.

Alex started spending a lot of time with Reverend McKnight and his son, T.P., and soon Trish and I became pretty good friends. She would call me from time to time to see if I was okay or needed anything. Because she was so nice, I began to feel bad for having an affair with her sorry ass husband. I only said he was sorry because the last time we slept together, he was married to her and told me all these horrible stories about her and how he wished he never married her, telling me how only got married because I was married, and he knew that he couldn't have me. I later found out that, in fact, Trish was a sweet lady and dedicated to her husband and her faith.

Being this is a small town, you know everyone was trying to find dirt about her and the only thing you could ever hear bad was that she said she wouldn't live in Camden if they built a mall and named it after her, which I don't blame her.

CHAPTER 8
UNTIL THE COWS COME HOME

The phone rang so much today I needed a secretary.

First was the mortgage person informing me I needed to make a payment real soon. Next, the telephone company, the cash advance folks, and, last but... not least, the car repo folks.

When Harry was living, he always made sure everything was paid. He would lay all the bills on the kitchen table, place a check with each one, and all I had to do was mail them off. Now, I placed the bills on the table in the kitchen and tried to figure out which ones I can pay this month. I knew I had to have my light bill, water and sewage, and money left for food, but it was eeny, meeny, miney, mo for the rest of the bills until I had no mo money.

I used to work as a teacher's assistant when Harry and I first got married, but after we started a family; Harry insisted I stay at home with the children. At first, I wasn't too sure about that, but I didn't argue with him because once Alex was born, I didn't want to leave him with anyone. I ended up being an at-home wife. As soon as I got Alex in school, Beany was born, and I was right back to square one.

For the last three months, I have been looking for work. I have had some good leads, but I have not found anything that pays the bills. I sometimes work with Trisha at the church daycare. It only pays a little over minimum wage, but it gives me something to do, and it helps me get use to working again.

Harry had insurance, but it only took care of his funeral and the bills over the last month. Now it's slowly running out and I must do something.

My life has really changed since Harry passed.

It started with the funeral.

Harry's Aunt Bertha May and Aunt Mer Liz showed up. These two ladies never came to visit us when he was alive. They had a chance to help raise Harry and Hiddy, but wanted no part, even knowing they had no other living relatives. They didn't even try to come to our wedding, and what's so bad about it was, they lived right there in Norfolk, VA, about an hour or so away.

They busted up in wake talking all loud and stupid.

"Girl, Harry had you up in here living good," Bertha May said. "I know you're going to miss him."

Then that ugly, fat ass Mer Liz said, "Mmm, she didn't miss him when he was living from what I heard."

They both walked into my kitchen.

"Girl, when was the last time you cleaned up this house?" they asked together.

Neither one offered any condolence. They just went on running their mouths. I felt like a little child being scorned by its stepmother. It seems as if they didn't care that we had company and that other people were listening to their dumb asses.

One-night, Teeny Baby was over.

"Why are you coming over here looking like you just came from a strip show?" Mer Liz said to her. Teeny looked at me.

"Girl, you better come over here and get these two fat bitches before I open their ass like a book and read them," Teeny Baby said.

"Teeny Baby," I said, "you are going to have to look over them. They can't help themselves."

"They got one more time to say something stupid and I'm going to beat some asses," Teeny Baby said. "They don't know me like that."

I was hoping they would say something else to Teeny Baby because I couldn't find it in me to say anything to them…

although I wanted too so badly. They never had anything good to say about anything I tried to do. They even had the nerve to accuse me of my husband's death. They both told Hiddy that I probably put some poison in his food or slipped something in his drink at the party we had that killed him. Hiddy didn't listen to them because she saw the results from the autopsy, which shows he died of a brain aneurysm.

Harry didn't like hospitals and, like most men around here, he was not getting physicals and worked until he dropped dead, which seems to be a rite of passage around here. On the night before the funeral, Bertha May and Mer Liz called me in the bedroom.

"It's been something I've been meaning to ask you," Bertha May said. "I'm not trying to get in your business, but what's this I heard about Alex not being Harry's son."

Now, out of all the messed-up things I've heard, that had to be the most inconsiderate thing I have ever heard, and without even thinking twice about it, I responded.

"I don't mean any harm," I said, "but you two fat bitches gots to get out of my house. How in the hell are the both of you fixing yall's mouth to ask me some shit like than. Yes, Alex is Harry's son and, furthermore, if he wasn't, what freakin' business is it of yours?"

Bertha May jumped off the bed.

"It's my damned business because Harry is my nephew and Alex is supposedly my great nephew, that's what business it is of mine," Bertha May said. "And, furthermore, I don't like your ass anyway. I saw your ass in Virginia about the time you called yourself having Harry's baby."

"You ain't seen nothing, you... fat blind bat," I said.

About that time, Teeny Baby entered the bedroom.

"What's all the noise?" she asked.

I explained myself and they were trying to explain their side of the incident.

"I told you old cows to fix your mouths and apparently you couldn't do that, so I'm going to have to mop the floor with one of ya'll ass up in here tonight. That is if you don't mind Beatrice," said Teeny Baby.
"Hell no," I said. "I'll help you kick their old asses."
I truly think we scared those two ladies to death because both broke for the door like we had pulled a gun on them. They did show up for the funeral but didn't ride in the cars with the little family Harry did have.

The next crazy thing that happened was somewhat of a nightmare. It seemed like every night for the past two weeks or so, the shed door would be found open, or I would hear something being kicked around in the garage. I had Officer Hutton ride past to check on me every now and then. I never went out to the shed since the little snake incident, but I would shut the door whenever I found it open. It was odd that the door would fly open. That door had a little latch on it, and when I shook it, it wouldn't even budge. Ma Elsie said whenever a door flew open or something just mysteriously fell, it was somebody you knew saying hello, so sometimes I would say, "Hi, Harry. Now could you please keep this door shut," knowing if he answered, he wouldn't have to worry about me shutting anything because the shed would be ashes when I was done with it.
Early Saturday morning, I decided to cut my own grass. Usually, I would get Lips to come over to cut it for me, but he had been missing lately. I got Alex up so he could go out to the shed with me to get the lawnmower. Alex, moving with the speed of a dew winged fly, slowly got out of bed, dressed, and met me at the shed. We both stood there like we were waiting

for the door to open by itself and the mower to just come out with Harry riding it, but that didn't and wasn't going to happen. Alex came up with an idea. On the count of three, he would hit the latch and I was to pull the door open.

One, two, three. The latch was pulled up and the door was swung back, and there it was, empty.

No mower.

The lawnmower was gone.

"Where's the mower, mom?"

"Alex, I haven't the slightest clue."

Alex and I went into the house, and I called our next-door neighbors to see if they saw anything. Nancy Perkins, who was probably the second nosiest person in the world, said, "Yeah. I saw one of Harry's friends put it on a truck."

"Are you sure, Nancy?" I asked.

"Yes. The big, lipped man that cuts your grass came over and got it one night."

I told her thanks, and then I called Lips' house, which he stayed with his mother, and asked about my mower. He told me he had borrowed it and that he was going to bring it over right away. Well, right away turned into no day because I never heard – head nor tail – from him.

One night at about eleven o'clock, someone was beating on my door. I cut on all the lights to see who it was. It was Lips banging, telling me to let him in. I immediately got on the phone and called Teeny Baby, Bucky, and Jr. Cefuss, being they all lived within a mile or so from me, to come over. Then, I called 911, which they kept me on the line while the Sheriff was being dispatched out to the house.

Alex asked did I want him to go get the gun from underneath my bed.

"No, I said, and how did you know it was a gun under the bed?"

"Beany told me daddy said that if we ever had a problem with Lips, the gun was under the bed," Alex replied.

"Why would your daddy tell Beany something like that?"

"I don't know. She just told me today when she talked to him," said Alex.

I didn't even ask another question. I just kept talking to 911 and pretended not to even believe that nonsense. The knocking stopped for a moment, and then he started beating on the garage door.

"Hey, Bitch! Let me in. I got something for your fine ass. I should have got that a long time ago. Harry! Harry wasn't hero either. He was screwing Teeny Baby right behind your back. Hell! How did you think he got that shit that time."

"Fuck you...you ugly crack head matha-fucka!" I yelled back. Now... I was trying my best not to curse around the children, but he was pushing it. Then I saw the lights coming up in the yard. It was Teeny Baby, Jr. Cefuss, Bucky, and Lucy Gay. What was so crazy was Lips didn't stop trying to get in the house.

Jr. Cefuss and Bucky tried to talk to Lips, but Lips wasn't trying to hear them.

"Girl, open this door," Teeny Baby said.

So, I opened the door. Right when Teeny Baby started to walk in, Lips grabbed her on the butt and Jr. Cefuss went off. He beat Lips' ass 'til the cows came home, and I know Lips must have felt like the cows were lost on the way home that night. I told the dispatcher I saw the police and that everything was under control and hung up the phone. Jr. Cefuss and Bucky dragged Lips behind the shed and when the police finally showed up, I told them my friends came over and Lips ran off. Of course, they said if I had any more problems, call them, but I knew I wouldn't have to worry about Lips anymore. I think he learned a lesson that night. Jr. Cefuss and Bucky had dragged

Lips behind the shed until the police left, then Bucky put him in the car and dropped him off, I mean physically dropped him off, at his house on the lawn and drove off. I never did see my lawnmower again, but neither did I see Lips again for a while. I guess he must be on that stuff like Harry implied.

For some odd reason, the door to the shed would still flay open sometimes. Once I even found the light on, and I said, "Keep the light off, Harry. The light bill is high enough." It seemed like I was starting to turn into Ma Elsie with all that back-water foo-doo crap.

Now the last thing that really put me through some changes was when my little Beany said, "Mommy, Daddy said when you yelled at Alex like that, you sounded like God when He was talking to Moses at the Burning Bush."

Now, I only said that about Harry when Harry was telling me something in a direct way. Even then, I said it inside my head. So how in the hell she came up with that beats me. I asked Beany why her daddy would tell her that, and she said, "God told him he did sound a little like Him when he used to be here." At this point, I was believing every word she was saying, and I was glad to hear Harry was in heaven.

After a while, I started sitting with Beany and asking her all kinds of stuff about her father. Beany and I became a lot closer because she enjoyed the fact, I listened to her talk about things she has seen and heard. I did mention to Beany if she got stuck in the TV, she'd better follow the light because the TV was going straight out the window. Beany said, "Mommy, my daddy said that he promises to keep the light off in the shed and that he's almost finished with the project he was working on."

"What project is that?" I asked.

"I don't know. He won't tell me, "Explained Beany.

One night, Alex came in my room and said Beany was talking something crazy and then left out the bedroom. He said he waited for her to come back in the room, but that's been a long time ago, and she's not in the house nowhere. I got out of the bed, cut on all the lights, and I searched the whole house looking for her. I even looked in her favorite little spot in the garage where she and Alex called their A and B sports bar, but she was nowhere to be found. Alex came up behind me.

"Look, mom," he said.

The shed was wide open, and the light was on. At first, it scared me because I could see a shape moving around in there. For a split second, I forgot all about my baby was missing and told Alex to lock the doors while I called 911. I soon snapped back yelling for Beany. Suddenly, a little head emerged from out of the shed. It was Beany's. I ran out there asking her what she was thinking about.

"Why were you out in the shed, Beany?" I asked.

"I was talking to daddy," cried Beany.

"From now on, you tell your daddy if he can't talk to you in the house, then he'd better get a cell phone and a pager so he can be contacted," I said.

"Don't he know that was dangerous to have you out in that shed this late at night." I went on arguing with Harry as if he was alive and well.

Beany never did go back to the shed after that, as far as I know, saying Harry was finished with his project. It also explained the light being on and the door being left open, which never happened again.

Things changed a lot since Harry's death, and yet I managed to keep going. In some ways, Harry managed to live on in spirit and through Alex and Beany, and especially through my little Beany.

CHAPTER 9
EVERY STAR IN THE SOLAR SYSTEM

Ma Elsie's porch was like a sanctuary. It seemed to bring out the warmest vibes. When I was a little girl, Ma Elsie and I would sit on the porch, and she would tell me stories about when she was a little girl. I would listen to each story and picture myself with her as she was helping her mother, Grandma Amy, in the garden, or when she was walking with her friends to school. Sometimes, I wished I were back in those days with her so that I could have had her as a best friend.

Seems like when we were on the porch, she could read my mind or tell me exactly what a mess I was making of myself. Ma Elsie could look at me and tell me precisely what I was up to... or what I was doing. I often wonder how she knows so much about me. It as if she followed me around, noting each thing I did, then recited it back to me on the porch.

***

This day, I went over to Ma Elsie's house with Alex and Beany. They both said that they missed Ma Elsie and that they wanted to spend the evening with her. For one, the children had just seen Ma Elsie two days ago, and two, they loved playing with that play station Ma Elsie had. I got the message. I knew why they really wanted to go over there. I had so much on my mind that the porch and Ma Elsie would be great therapy for me. Besides, I too wanted and needed an excuse to see Ma that day.

When we pulled up in the driveway, Ma Elsie was sitting on the porch as if she knew we were coming. I'm telling you this ESP psychic stuff was really taking its toll on me.

Alex and Beany jumped out of the car and ran to Ma Elsie and gave her the two biggest hugs I've ever seen. It was like they hadn't seen her in a year. The first thing Alex did was tell Ma Elsie about the lawnmower being stolen. Then he started talking about Lips trying to break in the house.

"I already know," Ma Elsie said. "Your mama told me all about it."

"Why don't you children go inside and play with your game," I said. Alex and Beany ran inside arguing over who was going to play what first. Ma Elsie placed her palmed right hand on my knee and put her left hand on my face. Then she leaned over and gave me the sweetest pampered kiss on the cheek. It reminded me of when I would hurt, and she kissed me to make it better. She asked how I was fairing.

"Fair," I said with a low undertone. "Ma, it's just so much happened or not happened right now. I sometimes don't know whether I'm coming or going, or if Harry is coming or going. Everyday, almost everyday, Beany tells Alex or me something that he was doing. She says things only Harry and I would know about. She even repeats things to me that I said to Harry in my head, but I have never said aloud to anyone. And the bad thing about it, Ma, is when Harry was living, I would have brushed all she would say out the door. Now, I want to and do believe every word she says. Ma, I find myself talking to Harry every night before I fall to sleep – and every time something falls, buzzes, cracks, or leaks. I'm telling Harry to stop. I even killed a fly the other day, and then cried for two hours telling Harry I'm sorry, thinking it just might have been him. Ma Elsie, am I going crazy?"

"No, baby," said Ma Elsie. "You are just grieving right now and you're doing it the only way you can, your way."

"I suppose."

"Just be thankful you have two sweet children that are there for you. How has Alex been doing, B.B.?" Ma Elsie asked.

"He's doing fine. His grades have fallen a little, but I expected that, but he is still making all B's. Whenever I ask if it is something he wants to talk about, he always says, 'No, I'm okay.'"

"I'll just keep an eye on that boy. Believe me, he's going through some things and grieving in his own way," Ma Elsie said. "You know that boy asked me one day was Harry his real daddy."

"What did you tell him, Ma Elsie?"

"What do you think?" Ma Elsie replied sarcastically, "I told him yes and I asked him why he would even ask such a thing like that."

"What did he say, Ma?"

"He said that his Aunt Bertha May and Aunt Mer Liz were in the room fussing because she said he wasn't Harry's son."

"He heard that?" I said with a frog as big as Raleigh in my throat.

"Why didn't he tell me, Mama?" I asked. "Why didn't you tell me he heard that?"

Ma Elsie just placed her hand back on my knee.

"B.B., you know I didn't put much thought into it being I knew the boy's Harry's son," she said. "I just reassured him and paid it no never mind." She paused.

"Yeah, I heard those rumors myself," said Ma Elsie, "But that boy has the blood of his father. I can tell it when I touch him. He feels just like Harry's blood."

Now, I didn't know what that meant, but I was glad to know she believed him to be Harry's.

Ma Elsie looked at me as if she was waiting for me to tell on myself. I knew she knew I was holding something back.

I mean, why wouldn't she know? We were on the porch after all. So, I explained to Mama what happened and why people were saying that Alex wasn't Harry's. I never told her who the man was that I had the affair with, but like the rest of this little country town, she already knew. Ma Elsie was the kind of woman that didn't straight out talk about sex or nothing like that, but every now and then, she would surprise me with a straight and forward question, and I guess this was the day for one of those questions.

"Did you use anything when you were with Reverend McKnight?" asked Ma Elsie.

"Mama! Why did you ask that?" I asked.

"Well, baby, you didn't sound so sure if you knew Alex was Harry's," replied Ma Elsie.

"Yes, Mom. Yes, I used protection. And who said it was Reverend McKnight?" I asked.

"Everyone in town that I cursed out when they told me." Said Ma Elsie.

"Well, everybody thinks they know everything about everybody. People make me sick. I wish everyone would just mind their own damned business. Mama, I'm getting so sick of hearing people talk about my children and me. I know who my son's daddy is!" I cried.

"Beatrice," Mama began, "you know this is a small town and everybody is in everyone else's business. You knew that when you slept with the man and let that be the last DAMN out of your mouth while to talking to me."

Then Ma Elsie started getting a little nosy asking me where I had met Tavone. I explained how I met him at ECSU, and then a couple years later we met again. He was attending Albemarle Bible College and things just happened. I then reminded Mama what Harry had given me on my anniversary.

"Yeah. You don't have to remind me of that. I loved that boy like he was my own son," confessed Ma Elsie, "but a man is a man, and sometimes you got to do what you got to do as a woman. You must take care of your own, baby...Take care of your own," Ma Elsie said softly as if she had been through some things herself.

Now, Ma Elsie, I love her dearly. She's my mother and my closest friend, but sometimes she could really get under my skin, and, like Harry, she despised Teeny Baby, saying, "She must can name every star in the solar system, as much as she has been on her back." Then she went on to say, "I heard about her, too."

"What did you hear about her Ma?" I asked.

"Well," said Ma Elsie, "I heard that she was the one that gave Harry the mess."

"Mama!"

"Now, I'm just telling what I heard."

"Who would tell you something like that, Ma Elsie?"

"Don't say nothing, but Ms. Nancy told me. Now, you know she works at the clinic. That's where she got the information."

"Ma, why didn't you tell me this a long time ago?" I asked. "I would have read her stinkin' ass. Sorry, Ma Elsie, but you know that I have done so much for her, that ho. Ma, why didn't you tell me?"

Ma Elsie explained that she had never interfered with my marriage or my business, and she felt at the time I probably couldn't handle it.

"Well, why are you deciding to tell me now, Mama?"

Ma looked at me through caring eyes.

"Beatrice, Baby, right now you only need positive people surrounding you, and I feel Teeny Baby is not anyone that can help you. With you being in the position you are in right now, you need to be concentrating on your children and your finances."

So that crazy, lying, sneaky, disease-having heifer slept with my husband while all the time I'm thinking Harry couldn't stand her guts, and he was in her guts. I was thinking to myself as Ma Elsie continued to explain the "that was then, and this was now" concept.

Ma Elsie also reminded me that I was just as wrong as Teeny Baby was, so I needed not to think about doing anything crazy.

That sneaky little bitch, Teeny Baby, I thought to myself. I don't mean no harm, but I wasn't trying to hear anything else Ma Elsie was trying to say. All I could do was think about all the things I've done with Teeny Baby.

I think Ma Elsie reached in her bra and pulled out a secret she shouldn't have shared with me because she tried several times to change the subject, but it didn't work.

It was getting late, and after talking with Mama all evening, I was ready to get home. I think I heard just about enough counseling for one day. I rounded up the children and we headed for home.

On the way home, all I could think about was Teeny Baby's trifling ass. I could see myself walking up her dirt path like Sophia on the Color Purple when she told Celie about Harpo beating her. I figured I would go home, get the children straight, and call her.

After the children were in the bed, I went in my room and got comfortable. I checked the messages. The first call was from none other than Teeny Baby, reminding me to try my dress on and to make sure to order my shoes by next Friday. Teeny Baby and Jr. Cefuss were getting married September 20th and I was Matron of Honor.

Insult to injury, Harry died on this date and Jr. Cefuss wanted to honor his life since Harry was his best friend.

I wanted to call her to set her straight, but something deep inside of me was already starting to forgive her. Maybe I kind of knew from the beginning, using that wife's instinct and gut feeling the psychics talk about. You know how you know the answer.

I prayed about it, and I asked God to help me through this with Teeny Baby. I decided to wait until I really thought everything over before I talked with her.

CHAPTER 10
COMPLICATION

Things were starting to get very spooky around here. Harry, or someone, had been placing things in strange places. I came home one evening and the shed door was open. An eight-track tape Harry loved to listen to was playing. Then one night, I don't know if I was dreaming or not, but I saw a shadow of a man standing right in from of my bed. I pulled the covers over my head and started saying the 23rd Psalm, sweating like I was under there cooking grits. When I pulled the covers from over my head, whatever I had seen was gone. I was afraid to get up and cut a light on, so I just slowly fell back to sleep.

I woke up that morning feeling as if I didn't sleep a wink. I dragged out of bed wondering whether it was a dream or what. I soon thought it may have been Lips. I immediately went to check on Alex and Beany to see if they were okay. I walked in their room, and Beany said with a sleepy voice, "Mom, did you see daddy last night standing over your bed?" Usually, I would have something smart to say, but this time I was speechless.

"Why is Harry doing this Beany? Did he say what he wanted?" I asked.

"No. Lately daddy hasn't been saying much of nothing, just standing around," Beany replied.

"If you see him before I do," I said hoping that I never see him until it's my time, "ask him why he is still here and what does he want."

Later that day, I continued to think about last night and what Beany said this morning. Now that I'm seeing ghosts, I feel it's time for a little help. I called Tavone and asked could we set up an appointment with him. Tavone told me I did not need to set up an appointment and to just come up to the office when I could. I took Beany over to Ma Elsie's. Alex had gone fishing with Bucky and Jr. Cefuss.

On the way over to his office at Shady Creek, I was kind of worried what people might say, but I had to talk to Tavone. Someone once said what you do wrong in the past may come back to haunt you, and I was starting to believe that Harry's soul was restless for some reason, and Tavone had just as much to do with this as I did. My only reason for talking to him is to clear up this rumor. I spoke to Trish. She was in the childcare area waiting for the last few parents to pick up their children. She asked me could I work any next week.

"Girl, just put me on the schedule and call me to let me know when," I said.

Trish was a very nice lady, and she loves Tavone to death. She told me if I needed anything to let her know.

"Thank you so much," I said.

"Reverend McKnight is in the office waiting for you," said Trish. "I'll let him know you are here."

"Thank you," I said.

As she walked back to get him, I couldn't help but look at her behind and thought to myself, "Damn, she's got a nice shape. If I was a man, I'd give the Rev a run for his money."

* * *

I think I was missing Teeny Baby so much that I was starting to think just like her because normally I wouldn't even think something like that. I believe I am going to call my buddy. She probably thinks I've lost my mind or something. When she leaves messages, I never return her calls.

One day she stopped by the house, and I acted like she was a bill collector. I cut off the TV and told the children to come in the room and be very quiet. Of course, Alex had a thousand questions, but I just put my hands over his mouth and told him I'll explain later. It's getting close to her wedding, and she was probably trying to figure out exactly what I was going to do, and why I haven't tried on my gown yet.

* * *

Trish came back into the daycare and told me Reverend McKnight was ready to see me. I walked into his office. Tavone stood to shake my hand.

"Hi, Beatrice Harold. So, what's up?"

The first thing that came out of my mouth was, "You tell me."

I could tell by the expression on his face that he was thinking, "Not this again," as he managed to smile.

"Tavone," I explained, "It's been some crazy things happening lately. We need to talk and be as honest as possible. The first thing I want to know is when we had sex, did you, in any way, tamper with the condom?"

"No, I did not," Tavone said. "Why would you think that?"

"Because a lot of people think that Alex looks a lot like you to the point, I'm starting to think the same thing. Then there's Beany. She tells me she used to see her Grand Ma Amy and this girl named Wendy, and they used to tell Alex to be strong. The girl named Wendy, Beany said, had a baby that wasn't born yet. Now, when Harry was living, I didn't pay that stuff much mind, but now with all that has happened, I can't help but believe some of what she is telling me. She even told Ma Elsie things about her Great Grandma Amy – and she has never seen Grandma Amy. Ma Elsie swears that everything she said about Grandma Amy was right on point. I could go on

101

with things she said or done that were right, which she could not have known. I could have sworn I saw something standing in front of my bed the other night that looked like a shadow of a man. The next morning, Beany asked me did I see her daddy standing in front of the bed. Something is going on and we need some answers."

Tavone just sat there with a distant look on his face. Then he said, "Do you remember when we were at the park, and you told me about Beany's encounters with the ghost or spirit named Wendy with the unborn child."

"Yeah, so?"

"Well, back when I met you, I was sleeping with a lot of women. Most of them were married. Anyway, I was with this one girl and her name just happened to be Wendy. She was married and her husband was impotent. She was totally in love with me and would have done anything for me. Well, she got pregnant by me. I didn't want her to keep the baby, so I arranged for her to have an abortion. It was done by this midwife I know. Anyway, she had complications and died. I don't know why or how this has anything to do with her talking to Beany, but when you told me about Beany seeing her, it scared me so bad that I couldn't sleep for weeks."

"Why didn't you tell me this before?" I asked.

"I actually tried to call you one night to tell you about this, but your answering machine would pick up and I would just hang up," Tavone said.

I forgot all about what I came for.

"You mean to tell me you were screwing all these women – and having sex with me?" I asked in disbelief. "Tavone, you are a real 'A' hole."

"Was!" Tavone said. "Was a real 'A' hole."

He was right. He did turn out to be a pretty nice man, and I figured that he didn't do anything that a nice looking, and single young man, wouldn't have done.

Although he was trying to change, he wasn't quite there yet. I guess he was trying to get the devil fully out of his system. I quickly returned to the problem at hand.

"Sorry about that, Tavone. I was a little out of line," I said.

"That's cool," Tavone said.

"Do you believe Harry is hanging around because he thinks Alex isn't his and he wants an explanation?" I asked.

"Maybe Harry thinks he knows Alex is his and is trying to contact you and let you know you don't have to worry about anything, and he loves you or something," Tavone said. Tavone went on to say maybe he will find a way of contact you through Beany and let you know what's wrong so you both can move on. Thinking about Teeny Baby and without using her name, I then told him about Harry and her messing around and how she was the one that gave Harry the STD.

"How old were we back then?" Tavone said. "Twenty, twenty-one? Beatrice, we were young. When you are young, you can't see things as clearly as you can when you're older. Back then, I think we all just lived for the moment because the moment was all we knew. We both are mature adults now, and when the past comes to visit, we tend to regret, so understand that it was as much Harry's fault as it was that lady's fault." Tavone then reached in his desk drawer and pulled out a line or two saying God forgives all, lets just learn to forgive ourselves.

He preached for a few more minutes, and then it was time for me to go. So, I thanked him for his time and promised to give him a call if something was to come up.

"You do that," he said.

I left out feeling like we were still lying to each other and ourselves because there were a lot of reasons Harry could be hanging around the house.

Like always.

Tavone wasn't going to go there if I didn't.

I picked up the children and headed back home.

Alex and Beany were tired, so they fell to sleep on the way home.

For the first time in months, I looked at my surroundings and noticed the sky, for some reason, seemed a little bluer. The tree line showed an image of God's great craft and I realized everything happened in my life has happened for a reason. I thanked God for the epiphany, and when we arrived home, I opened myself to the idea that forgiveness of self would be the only way to learn to forgive others.

Once I got myself straight and the children to bed, I prayed and then picked up the phone to call Teeny Baby.

The phone rang about three or four times. In some ways, I was hoping she didn't pick up so I could have a few more minutes to get my thoughts together. Then it happened.

"Hello?"

"Hey, Teeny Baby. This is B.B."

"Yeah right." Then she hung up.

Not wasting a second, I redialed the number.

"Hello?" she answered.

"Girl, you had better not hang up on me again."

"What's up?" she said and then laughed. "What in the hell have you been doing? I've tried to call you a thousand times with no luck. I thought you were going through some kind of breakdown. I started to send the FBI around there to make sure you haven't offed the children and then yourself."

Teeny rattled her trap on and on, not even stopping to take a breath or to let me answer any of her foolish but understandable questions.

I couldn't help but get right to the point, so I asked the big question. There would be no beating around the bush for me, straight direct and forward with it.

"Teeny Baby," I asked sounding like God when he was talking to Moses at the burning bush, "did you sleep with Harry? And don't lie to me either girl."

At first, Teeny Baby denied it, but she was stuttering so hard while she was talking, I thought for a minute she had swallowed Porky Pig.

"Why are you lying, Teeny Baby?" I asked. "I know you did, and I'm already over it. I'm only asking you so I can help put closure to all the crazy things that's been going on in my life. All I wanted to know is did you, and if you did, why?"

I could tell Teeny Baby was crying because she was blowing her nose so hard, I went to the door to make sure there wasn't anyone driving up blowing their horn.

"B.B., I'm sorry. I'm so sorry," cried Teeny Baby.

"Teeny Baby, all I wanted to know is why?"

"Honestly, Beatrice, I was so jealous of you and Harry. It seemed like you two were so happy, and there I was going out every night pretending I didn't want a man. All the time I was wishing I had what you had, not so much Harry, just someone like him."

"So, while I was wishing I was single, you wanted to be in my shoes?"

"Beatrice, do you remember I used to tell you I was looking for a husband whenever you and I went out?"

"Yes," I replied, with my mouth twisted like I was sucking on a Sour Ball.

"Deep inside, I meant it, knowing I wasn't going to find anything good in a damned night club."

She went explaining herself, but nothing she said really gave me the answer I wanted to hear. So, I said, "Why Harry?

He was my husband, and you are and always will be my best friend. How could you be with him?"

"Beatrice, I don't know. Maybe I was trying to mess up the good thing you and Harry had so you would spend more time with me. Hell, I don't know."

"How did it happen? How did you and Harry hook up?" I asked. Half of me wanted to know and the other half of me was asking why I wanted to know.

Teeny Baby began to explain the events that took place.

"Harry came over to my house the day before yall's anniversary. He wanted to know if I knew what kind of flowers to get and would I order them for him. I could see the love for you in his eyes and it tore me up with envy. I was so jealous of you that I, being the mental case I am, wanted to test his love for you. Maybe in my own sick, sadistic way, I thought I was doing my best friend a favor, to see if he would fall for the trap and cheat. When he asked me would I do this for him and I said, yes, if you do something for me.

"Harry being eager to get the flowers said, 'What do you need sis?'

"I said, 'Yeah, now I am your sister,' and Harry said, 'What do you need?' I then asked him to f--k me, and at the same time I started rubbing on him. I went down on him. He was trying to pull away, but I kept being persistence. I could see that he was very uncomfortable because by time I started working on that long big...

"Stop!" I told her.

I now really understood this chick was as off the rocker as Forest Gump at a science fair. I mean she was just talking to me like I was asking her about someone she use to sleep around with I didn't know.

"Teeny Baby, I didn't need to hear all of that."

106

"I am so sorry. You know I'm a few eggs short of a dozen," said Teen Baby.

"A few eggs? Try a whole dozen short of a dozen," I said.

We talked on the subject for about thirty minutes with Teeny Baby either begging for forgiveness or saying she's sorry every five seconds.

We caught up on lost time, and I promised I was going to take care of my part as far as the wedding goes. She asked was I still going to be her Matron of Honor.

"Girl," I said. "All the stuff we've been through. I wouldn't have it any other way". After I had talked to Teeny Baby, I felt a whole lot better for some reason. Maybe it's because Teeny Baby said that she could tell that Harry felt bad about the whole situation. When I asked her about the STD, she said she didn't know until Harry told her he had it. I guess you live and learn.

I'm still learning.

I wasn't at all sleepy and it was going on about one thirty. I hadn't written in my journal in quite some time, so I went in my closet and pulled out a box where I kept all my little secrets. I didn't feel too much like writing. I kept looking through until I ran across the book Black Frame. I remembered reading it all the time, especially when I felt a little out of place in my life. I flipped through the pages, smiling as I came across different poems. Some of them reminded me of certain things I was going through at special times in my life. Tonight, I came upon a poem that for a long time I couldn't understand until Harry passed. Now it's all clear to me. I think the poet was saying, once you have prayed, you leave everything else in God's hands. The most important begging you could ever do involves a prayer said for your soul, that it may enter heaven's eternal love. From the day I was born, somebody prayed for me. Even after I could pray for myself, somebody prayed for me. And before I take my last breath, I would have already begged God to release me from all the sins of this sometimes-sad world. I've always believed prayer was a way of begging God for anything you wanted and thanking Him for what you needed. If you were positively sure everything would go your way, and everything you simply ask God for you would have, begging God wouldn't even be necessary and heaven would really be right here on earth. I feel the poet understood that, and that he had experienced something in his life that makes him thank God for the greatest gifts in the universe and for the promises of life after life. I began to read:

'Turn to You'

When I no longer feel
the wind dancing on my face
Somehow, I see my future
And it seemed so out of place
That's when I turn to you
And asked you for that missing time
So that I could have the strength
To leave yesterday behind

When I no longer feel the sun
Massaging me on my back
And tomorrow I see future
And it has slipped through the cracks
That is when I turn to you
To ask you for your hand
So that I might have the wisdom
To understand one day

When I no longer feel the rain
Falling softly on my skin
That is when I turn to you
And beg you to let me in

And when I no longer take that breath
You have given me at my birth
I would have already turned to you
To release me from this earth.

It just makes me wonder if Harry doesn't want to move on. I seem to feel something different from this each time I read it. As I flipped through the pages, I noticed the last poem in the book was missing. I went back to the contents and saw it was the poem "Feeling Me." I didn't remember tearing that page from the book. I had glanced through the book several times since Harry passed but I can't recall it missing until now. Maybe Alex or Beany was going through my stuff and ripped the page, so they just tore it out. I'll get those rascals tomorrow.

I put Black Frame back in the box. I was too lazy to get out of bed to put it in the closet, so I just cut the light off and fell to sleep with the box on the other side of the bed.

When I woke in the morning the box was back in the closet. I didn't even bother to give light to why or how.

CHAPTER 11
TWILIGHT ZONE STUFF

It was the hottest morning ever recorded in Camden. I lived on North River Road, which they say a river once ran through, and I'm telling you, the sun was beaming rays that would have dried any river that ever passed through here.

Teeny Baby had called me at 5:30 in the morning asking me if I would go with her to Little Times. She wanted to know if I would help her find something to wear for their honeymoon.

"Sure, I would love to," I said, "but the place doesn't open until 9:00. And why are you calling so early?"

"Girl, this is my wedding day and I'm so nervous that I can't sleep," Teeny Baby said.

"What are you so nervous for? You've been dating him for going on three years, and you two practically live together."

"Beatrice," Teeny Baby said, "you know I'm not the marrying type. I just might end up finding someone while I'm married and start breaking my back behind Jr.'s back. And just suppose he finds out that I had an affair with his best friend. He might leave me."

"Stop," I said. "Teeny Baby, do you love the man?"

"Yes, I love him but…"

"But nothing. Love is all you need. Now, I'm going to sleep. Call me at eight."

I know I had to have been in a sleep deeper than the ocean when the phone rang. It was Teeny Baby. Again.

"Hey girl. It's eight o'clock. Rise and shine," said Teeny Baby.

"Okay," I said and then hung up. I put the phone on mute and went back to sleep.

Two seconds later, the doorbell rang and rang and rang. I got up and there she was. At the door smiling like a Cheshire cat. We dropped the kids off at Ma Elsie's and headed to Little Times. For the first time I can remember, Teeny Baby was buying her own lingerie, and I was helping pick it out. We settled for a red hot all access, ass and tits out negligee. For some reason, that girl loved red. Maybe it was the devil in her.

"I hope you don't hurt that man tonight," I said.

"Girl, I'm going to pull off that thing until it was it's raw."

I reminded her how small she said his thing was and that she didn't want to shrink it even more. Teeny Baby got quiet for a moment.

"You see," she said, "that's what I'm afraid of. In a year or so, I may have an urge for a foot long hot dog instead of a Vienna sausage."

I told her if she does, I would go with her to Wal-Mart and we can buy whatever she needed, because I'm not going to let her mess up like I did. Teeny Baby hugged me.

"B.B., I love you so much. You're like the big sister I never had." She started crying as she hugged me. All I could do was cry and hug her back, reassuring her that I loved her also.

We left Little Times and headed straight to Wal-Mart. She said she needed some bedroom slippers. Although she had got some nice and sexy ones from Little Times, she claimed they were uncomfortable, and she wasn't going to try to impress Jr. Cefuss and pop a corn. She wore so many pumps I think she had a corn on every toe, even her big toe.

Like always, our time was limited, so we got what we needed and went on our way. We stopped and picked up the kids and headed for home. We arrived at the church at ten o'clock. Ma Elsie was in charge of getting the bride, the bridesmaid, the flower girl, and the Matron of Honor ready.

Bucky, Jr. Cefuss, Lips and Knotts were all in the other room getting dressed. Knotts and Lips were both in the wedding. Knotts was the best man and Lips was one of the groomsmen. Lips, I hadn't seen since the incident and didn't care to see, but he was one of Jr. Cefuss' best friends, so I had to deal with him. Hell, he's the one who would escort me down the aisle.

The only real problem I had was Lucy Gray.

I couldn't figure out for the life of me, why Teeny Baby picked Lucy Gray for one of her bridesmaids. When I asked her, she said she needed a body.

The wedding was beautiful.

Bucky, Lips, and Jr. Cefuss didn't even look like themselves. They say black makes you look smaller, and Lips' lips looked a little smaller. When Lips walked me down the aisle, I wasn't worried about tripping or falling. I was more worried about laughing. I swear them things are big.

The music stopped; we were all in our places. Then started the old, "We are gathered here today." There I was standing beside my best friend, the lady who slept with my husband, standing next to my husband's best friends, standing next to the man that makes me laugh, stole my lawnmower, and tried to break in my house. Yet, this was the most beautiful day I have seen in a long time.

At the reception, I just knew there was going to be some crazy stuff going on with Bucky and Lips in the same room as alcohol being served. And they didn't let me down. It started when Lips began drinking like someone said, "No more drinking after today." I mean he was really guzzling them down. As soon as he reached his peak, Lips said, "Hey! Ain't it my turn to dance with the ho?"

Bucky surprisedly didn't drink anything, so he was the one that tried to defuse the situation. Jr. Cefuss took off his jacket and was rolling sleeves up preparing to rumble. Knotts was all muscular and everything, but he was as heartless as the tin man on the Wizard of Oz.

I guess Knotts and Lucy Gray were a couple, so Knotts had to find courage from somewhere, so he called Lips over to the side, talking calmly, and then hit Lips so hard Lips passed out and pissed on himself at the same time. Knotts then asked me if I would call a cab, but no cabs ran on Sunday or Monday or anytime, I took a chance and called Mr. John D. He answered. I asked if he would come to Bourbon Street Community Center to take Lips home. I explained how he was, being obnoxious, he agreed but I could hear his grandchildren in the background saying, "Hell naw, he ain't going nowhere," so I said quickly, "I'll pay you thirty-five dollars for the favor." He hung right up.

Five minutes later, John D. arrived. The fellas put Lips in the car and paid Mr. John D. John D. threw his hands up, waving, with a "Thank ya, thank ya." We didn't worry about Mr. John D. being safe because everyone in Camden knows not to mess with him whether they were sober or drunk. That would be like signing a death warrant.

The reception went on as if nothing ever happened, and we did the electric slide until my heels were ground down like flats. Alex and Beany had the most fun the way they danced and jumped around. It's been a long time since my children, and I had this much fun.

We got home at about 9:30 p.m. Alex and Beany were knocked out. Knotts and Lucy Gray followed me home to make sure I got there safe. I was glad they did follow me because I needed Knotts to help me take the children in the house. I was tired, too. I took a quick shower and went to bed. I remembered that I had left the fan in the window, so I got up to take it out and to lock the window back down. The house had cooled down from about a hundred degrees to ninety-eight degrees. I was definitely going to make sure to call the man fixing it so he could be out here first thing tomorrow morning.

I was so tired that as soon as my head hit the pillow, I was out like a light. Either I was dreaming, or I was losing my mind, but it had gotten so cold in the house that my nose hairs were frozen. I sat up in bed. As I was breathing, I could see smoke coming from my mouth. I tried to get up so I could go check on the children, but my legs were stuck to the mattress like they were frozen as well.

All of a sudden, I heard a loud humming noise coming darned from the living room. It sounded like the television was left on. I knew ed well I didn't cut on the TV, but the strange thing was the sound was moving or coming closer to my room. Next, I started seeing a glow or bright light. I was so scared that I lost any water that was in me. I tried to move, but it was like I was frozen solid to the bed. As the light got closer, I started praying harder than the priest on the Exorcist. I was hoping maybe the air conditioner man had come over to the house and fixed the air while I was sleep.

I always sleep with my bedroom door open so I can hear the children in case they fall out of bed or something, but I had no intention of experiencing something like this. Suddenly, there she was, walking in my bedroom, glowing brighter than the lights at the Camden High School football field.

I asked her why she was in here, what was wrong, but she gave me no answer. Maybe she didn't answer because although I was talking, not one sound came out of my mouth. Beany began to talk, but it wasn't her voice coming out. It sounded just like Harry talking.

"Beatrice," she said, "I think it's time. Look in my Duke jacket on the inside pocket. You will find a key. Take that key and go out to the shed. In the shed you will see a cubby hole with a box in it."

I was so out of my mind; all I could do was sit there and let the tears flow down my face. Beany just stood there after .

she said that she started to reach out for me, yet I couldn't move to reach for her. The phone rang. I knew I couldn't move, but I tried, and, to my surprise, I reached right over my nightstand and picked up the phone keeping my eyes on Beany standing there glowing like a space alien.

"Hello?" again being surprised that I could talk.

It was Ma Elsie on the line. Beany turned around and walked out of the room.

"Ma Elsie, I'll call you right back," I said, and then hung up. For some odd reason, it was back hot as hell, and I was moving faster than Carl Lewis at a track meet. I ran to the children's bedroom to see if Beany was okay. Both Alex and Beany was in bed. Beany was holding her teddy bear and laying in the same position she was in when I placed her in bed. I thought maybe she was sleep walking, but that still couldn't explain the cold air, the noise sounding like a TV was on, and the bright ass light I saw glowing around her earlier.

I didn't know what to do, so I cut on every light in the house. Then I picked up the phone to return Ma Elsie's phone call. The phone rang, but she was not answering. I got a little worried because she had just called me ten minutes ago.

I called Officer Hutton to see if she would drive by and check on Ma Elsie to make sure she was okay. I continued to call her, but I got no answer. Soon, the phone rang. It was Ma Elsie.

"What in the world are you doing calling me this early in the morning? B.B., are you out of your mind? Something better be wrong, having the police peeping all in my windows and banging on my door just because I didn't answer the phone. You know I ain't gonna answer the phone this early", said Ma Elsie.

"But, mama, you called not more than ten minutes before I called you. I was just returning your call," I said.

"Beatrice, I did not call you. As a matter of fact, someone kept calling me and hanging up, so I cut the ringer off," Ma Elsie explained.

I told what happened and how when the phone rang, I was able to answer, and how I couldn't move before then, and the caller said they were you, and that's why I called.

"Look, Beatrice," Ma Elsie said, with a little attitude, "call me later and we'll talk. The children are fine, aren't they?"

"Yes."

"Well, I will call you back later," and she hung up. Ma Elsie didn't like getting up early in the morning and if you disturbed her, she would literally bite your head right off. Okay. Now Ma Elsie said that she didn't call, Beany was in the bed like nothing ever happened. The house was back hot as hell, and I was standing in the middle of the living room totally confused.

I decided going back to sleep was out of the question. I went to reach for the remote control to see what was on TV until I thought about that sound and figured that was also out of the question. I cut on the radio instead, stretching out on the couch hoping I could catch a little shuteye. The phone rang.

"Hello?"

"Beatrice, is this you?"

"Yes. You called my number, didn't you?" I answered with a little relief.

"I think we need to talk," said Tavone.

"I also think the same thing."

"You wouldn't believe what happened to me this morning about 2:30."

"Where are you?" I asked.

"I'm at church in my office. Why?" Tavone asked.

"I'll call you right back," then I hung up.

I figured if Ma Elsie didn't call, maybe this isn't Reverend McKnight on the other line either. I waited about ten minutes, and then I called back to his office and was relieved when he answered.

"Beatrice?"

"Yes."

"Look, we need to come clean with each other. I know we promised to never bring this up, but after last night, we have got to straighten this mess out once and for all," Tavone explained with a trembling voice.

"What happened? Why are you calling me, talking about straightening something out? Straighten out what?"

"Look, last night I was in my studying quarters. Sometimes if I am tired, I'll fall asleep in there. Well, I woke up freezing my behind off. I know I wasn't dreaming. I heard someone or something saying, 'The word, not the man.' It sounded like the chipmunks. I mean, it was a very scary sound. I tried to get up out of the chair to see if someone was there, but I couldn't move. The closer the sound got, the deeper the voice was getting. The sound went from a high pitch to a very low tone, kind of dragging. Then, it was the bright light almost blinding me."

"Did you see anything else?" I asked.

"Yes," said Tavone. "It was your Beany."

"My Beany?"

"Yes, Beany. She walked right in the door and started talking fast again, but as fast as she was talking, I could understand every word she was saying."

"What did she say?"

"She was saying everything I've ever promised a woman and never came through with. She was even sounding like each woman as she talked. But the one thing I remember the most and the last thing she said to me was 'Do what you know is right,' and then she started reaching out for me, but I couldn't move. The phone started ringing and as I reached to answer, I suddenly was able to move. It was your Ma Elsie, but she wouldn't say anything but, 'Hello. this is Ma Elsie.' When I tried to answer her, it was like she couldn't hear me. I tried to

117

call her back, but the phone just kept ringing. Beany turned and walked away as I held the phone. The next thing I know, everything was back to normal."

As Tavone rattled on about his experience, all I could do was sit there and pray all this was a dream.

"Beatrice, do you hear me?" Tavone asked.

"Yes, I heard you, but I don't know what to say because I had the same experience at about the same time as you were having yours."

"You mean to tell me this happened to you at the same time as I was going through this?" asked Tavone.

"Yes."

"What did she say to you?"

"All she said was for me to open some box in Harry's tool shed."

Tavone was quiet on the other end. He finally asked me the question that I knew he was going to ask when he first called.

"Beatrice, did you get the test back?"

I paused for a moment.

"What test?" I asked. "What are you talking about?"

"Beatrice, I know you have tried to block this out of your mind for all these years, but we have to come clean with this because I can't be going through this everyday. I'll go crazy and so will you. I am telling you Harry's soul isn't at rest and he apparently knows something, and we need to do something before the spirit starts getting violent, and starts hurting people, maybe even Alex, Beany, or us," Tavone pleaded with me.

After five and a half years of never bringing this up to anyone, not even to myself, I finally came face to face with the truth, and the truth was Tavone, and I had a one-night thing once when Harry and Alex went to see Hiddy in Goldsboro. I was upset because he chose my birthday weekend to go instead of doing something I wanted to do. I refused to ride to Goldsboro with him, so he left with Alex, leaving me behind.

I never meant to have sex with Tavone, but he knew I was vulnerable and, being the dog he was, he took advantage of a bad situation. The next thing I knew, I was walking around pregnant with Beany. I wanted Beany to be Harry's so bad that I pretended Tavone and I never happened. Tavone was just the opposite. He insisted that we get a blood test and swore if anything did happen and Beany turned out to be his, he was going to take care of her. But like all the other promises that he made, he took the blood test and afterwards, I never heard from him again. So, while he was on the phone talking about all the drama he was going through this morning, I was like "good for your ass. You should have been seeing more than that."

"Tavone, what do you want me to say? Yeah, I know what happened. Beany is yours."

"What?" he asked.

"Tavone, you supposedly got the results, and you were the one that was going to do so much, and all of a sudden, I don't hear from you about the situation until now."

"Look, Beatrice," Tavone said, "I never received a letter telling me the results, so I figured that everything was all gravy. Apparently, things are more complex than I thought."

"So, what do you suggest we do?" I asked Tavone. "You're the Reverend Tavone McKnight almighty, aren't you?" I said sarcastically.

"The first thing we need to do is to find out if either of your children are mine because I've heard the rumors, just like you, about Alex being mine," Tavone said.

"And just how are you going to that?"

"I will go to get a blood test, and you can bring Alex and Beany later that day so they can give samples, pretty much the same as we did before."

119

Now, Tavone had all the answers, but for insurance, I asked him just what he was going to do if either of the children are his. Of course, Tavone had all the right answers, so he promised to take care of them. Damn, one thing about Tavone, he could make some promises, but keeping them aren't on his list of things to do.

We talked for an hour on the phone about everything that took place that morning and how we were going to arrange our little meeting. When I hung up, I didn't feel any better than I was feeling before he called. By the time I was able to sleep, Alex and Beany were wide awake. I had to get up and cook breakfast.

In two weeks, the children started back to school, and I was left trying to figure out how I was going to buy school clothes. If either of those children of mine are Tavone's, I am just going to have to make him pay. Maybe that's why this haunting Harry stuff is happening. Harry might be trying to help.

"Girl, stop tripping," I told myself. "You are just trying to make that man pay for all the lies he's told." Then I asked myself what's wrong with that?

Ma Elsie called at about 11 a.m.

"Beatrice are you feeling any better?" she asked.

"Yeah, Ma. I'm just so tired. I never thought in a million years I'd be going through something like this. I mean, this is some twilight zone stuff happening, Ma, and it's taking its toll on me."

"Maybe you need to listen to whatever the entity was trying to tell you. What did it say?" Ma Elsie said.

I explained to her what it said again.

"Well, what are you waiting on?" Ma Elsie said. "Go check it out, see what it's trying to show you." I thought about it hard, and it only made sense, so I told Ma that I was going to look for it later.

The children asked if they could go to the pool today, and I told them once the man came to fix the air conditioner we could head out. I instructed the children to go straight to their rooms while I fixed lunch for the outing. The house was still hot as a bucket of fried gizzards. I called Pacos to make sure they were still coming out to fix the air conditioner, and they assured me someone was on the way.

I started straightening up around the house. While I was cleaning the bedroom, I decided to look in Harry's jacket for the key. I reached in the inside pocket hoping nothing was in there, but there it was: a key, and it looked just like a key that would go to a box. Normally, I would have been afraid, but last night scared me so bad, I was willing to do anything to stop all the madness. I was ready to check this thing out. I went to get Alex and Beany and headed straight to the shed. Once at the shed, I came back to earth because I was right back scared.

"Mom, we can count to three and do out little routine," Alex said.

"Okay," I said.

Beany walked over, unlocked the latch, and walked right in.

"See mommy, it's okay. Ain't nothing going to bother you in here. You looking for that box, ain't ya, Mom."

"Yes. How do you know?"

"Because daddy said he talked to you last night," Beany said with a beautiful little smile on her face.

"Yeah, 'cause I heard him," Alex said, and then started laughing.

"You ain't heard nothing," said Beany.

"How do you know what I heard?" Alex said as he continued to laugh.

"Now, ya'll two knock it off. Alex... get me that ladder over there."

"I'll get the box for you mom," said Alex.

Alex placed the ladder on the wall and retrieved the box from the cubbyhole, just where Harry, or whoever, said it would be.

"Mom, are you going to open it," said Beany and Alex.

"No," I said, "I'll open it later," fearing what might be inside.

I carried the box inside and put it on the counter in the kitchen. I wanted to wait until I was by myself to open it, but I couldn't. I just had to see what was in it. Curiosity was killing me. I told Alex and Beany to go in the living room and watch cartoons, while I got dressed. They knew I wouldn't be long, so they happily agreed to watch cartoons. I think they also wanted to know what was in the box as much as I did. As the children went to watch TV, I yelled to Beany not to sit right in front of it, thinking how I didn't need any more drama than I've already had today.

I took the key with my hand shaking like I was going into shock. I began to turn the key. The box opened. The first thing I saw in the box was pictures. The first one was an old one of Harry and me when we first started dating. The second picture was of me pregnant with Beany, but the last picture had me puzzle. It was a picture of me standing at Harry's burial site. Beside me was Beany and Alex, and unless Harry has a twin, it was a man standing behind me with his hands on both Alex and Beany's shoulders.

I placed the picture on the bed and reached back in the box and pulled out envelopes. The first envelope was the poem "Feeling Me," the same poem that was missing from my **Black Frame** book of poetry. I started to read it, hoping I would find some message in it that would give me some type of explanation.

Feeling Me

When you feel someone

You tend to feel their happiness
The happiness that captures the very essence
Of what is beautiful about that someone
And all you wish
Is that someone you feel knew
Just how much you are feeling them
When you feel someone
You feel their pain
The pain that claws at their heart
Like a furious lion in a cage of hurt
And all you wish
Is the someone you feel
Knew how much you were really feeling them

When you feel someone
*   I mean really feel someone*
*   You're really feeling me*
*   Ya feel*

I tried to feel this, but I wasn't feeling him...at all. All I felt was fright. I rushed to the next envelope. I ripped it open. It was a letter from Harry. It read:

Dear Beatrice,
*   If you're reading this letter that means I'm either dead or you are doing something you're not supposed to be doing, being sneaky. Any who, I'm writing to let you know that I understand, and I forgive you. I shouldn't have done what I did. When I went into the marriage, I wasn't taking the vows as seriously as I should have, but I can say even with all the problems I may have caused, I have always and will always love you. You...doing what you did can only be understandable because I would have probably reacted in an even worse way. I have and always will take care of you and the children even in my death. I will make sure you and the children are well taken care of. What I need you to do*

123

first is open each envelope in the order that they are marked. Second, make sure you follow the instructions in the other envelope. And last, don't let him walk away scott free. Make him do his part. Tell him to do what is right. I will not rest until I feel things are in order.

 Love,
 Harry
 P.S. Whatever you do, don't tell him about this letter. He will do his part.

 P.P.S. Tell Alex to be strong. Tell Beany I'll talk to her later.

  I knew I would read this letter about fifty more times, so I went straight for the next envelope. The next one was inside of a larger envelope. I opened it. It was a letter from the social services department dated May 18, 1990, about the same date Tavone and I had taken a paternity test. Inside was a note from Harry saying simply, "He knows already." I opened the letter which read: "The test results show that there is 99.9% chance of accuracy that Tavone P. McKnight is the father of Breanna LaToya Harold."

  I started crying with hurt and shame. I had a pain in my heart that ran all over my body. How was I going to explain this to Beany? I wondered did she already know. How long did Harry know this? The who, what, when, where and how ran through my mind faster than the speed of light. I started to curse Harry for keeping this from me all these years. I wanted to blame him for everything. If he hadn't started his stuff, I would have never started mine.

  Alex and Beany knocked on the door and asked if I was okay.

  "Yes. I'm just crying because I miss your daddy." I then told them to go back into the living room and watch TV. I pulled myself together enough to open the last envelope.

It was another letter from Harry that read:

Beatrice, if you are feeling the pain and the hurt that I'm feeling right now, then you're really feeling me.

I was definitely feeling him, and now I understood where he was going with the poem. Now, I was just waiting for the happiness. The letter went on to say,

I set aside a little something to make sure you and the children wouldn't have to go without while you pieced your life back together. You will find it in the last envelope you open. But listen closely; do not let this man know that you received anything. If he doesn't step up to the plate, he will hear from me because I won't rest until he does. A man is a man, and a man takes care of his responsibilities. For no child has ever asked to be born. I know there is a lot of questions in your head right now, but in time you will piece this puzzle together because every footprint leaves a trail, and every trail leads to somewhere. You just have to know where you are going and what you hope to find. Love, Harry

After wiping more tears from my eyes, I opened the last of the five envelopes. To my surprise, it was an insurance policy for one hundred and fifty thousand dollars. It was dated October 16, 2001, five months before Harry died, which was the same month we went to see Hiddy. The contract was drawn up in Goldsboro and was signed with my name on it. There was a letter folded up in the contract.

Beatrice, you know I always believed that Beany had a special gift. She once told me that Great Grand Ma Amy said she'll see me soon. I don't believe she knew what it meant, but I told her never to tell you what she was telling

me because you would throw the TV out the window. So, I've been preparing to meet them. For me, preparing meant making sure you guys were taken care of. If you're reading this letter, that means I'm with my mommy and daddy. I love you.

Love, Harry

After reading everything, I placed it all in the order I found it and put the box in the closet. Alex came to the door and asked if we were ready to go yet.

"Yes," I said. "Just give mommy a few more minutes."

We got everything together and headed for the pool. On the way, I was thinking maybe I should drop the children off at Ma Elsie's and drop myself off at Cherry, a mental hospital in Goldsboro. Everything you could imagine going through your head was going through my mind. But one thing was certain, I knew now more than ever before that Harry loved me to death. The only thing was that his loving me to death was starting to kill me. Knowing he loved me like he does, I'm just wondering why he went this route. He knows everything scares me, yet he was using Beany to get his point across when he could have told me all of this when he was in the flesh. I guess I wouldn't have wanted to listen. Come to think of it, maybe in some crazy, deranged way, it's better like this. Plus, Harry was always good at solving problems.

Now it was time for the Reverend Tavone McKnight to do his part.

126

CHAPTER 12
4th SUNDAY IN THE DIRTY

"You've got to ask someone greater than me," Ma Elsie would say when I asked her a question, she didn't have the answer to. All I wanted to know is would the hurting ever stop.

It was December, Harry's favorite month. He would work double over time to make sure the children got what they wanted. He was also in charge of putting up those horrible lights outside. I hated them, but the children loved them and that's all that mattered to Harry. Alex had already gone to the shed and started dragging out the Christmas boxes, asking if he could put them up this year. Alex was now eleven years old, and since the last year, he has always helped me put them up. I figured I would let him do the lights this year – all by himself. Alex's birthday was also in December, and he was soon to be a teenager. Which meant I really need Harry now more than ever.

Jr. Cefuss and sometimes Bucky would come over and take Alex fishing or to a basketball game, but for some reason, Alex didn't take to those guys too good. For some odd reason, he took to Tavone, but Tavone only took him and T.P. to baseball practice or to a game they had. Like always, Tavone was still making promises he couldn't, or simply wasn't going to, keep. After his little scare with the ghost of Harry's passing, he started doing little things for Beany like giving her a dollar or two when he saw her, or buying something on her birthday and whatever, but he was a long way from being a father to her. Part of the reason is because Trish didn't accept Beany at all. When she found out about Beany, she first confronted me and told me I was no longer needed at the daycare. At times, she would even call to my house and hang up. She came with Tavone whenever he came to pick up Alex for practice.

Tavone was trying to keep the peace, I guess.

Alex's birthday was Saturday. Bucky, Jr. Cefuss, Knotts, and Lucy Gray was giving Alex a party at the skating rink. No one knew that Harry had a big insurance policy set aside for me, so they were all pitching in to help.

Alex must have invited every kid from his school because it seemed like the whole sixth-grade class was there.

The people he wanted most to come didn't show up, Tavone and T.P. Alex kept asking me was I sure I gave them the invitation. I felt bad because even Beany was looking forward to seeing them as well. After Alex's party, we went home. We were all beat from skating. I put the children to bed. Then I called Teeny Baby because it was time for a little revenge. Nobody gets away with disappointing my children like that. I never asked anything of Tavone after we found that Beany was his.

As a matter of fact, I figured that the only thing that Harry wanted from Tavone was for him in some way to be there to support Alex and Beany. And Tavone was failing that badly. Along with that, Tavone has done a lot of women wrong. I don't think he fully understands just how much damage he has done to women over the years, and it was about time for his past to catch up with him. I figured it was time to make him a little more responsible and a little more aware.

If he knew he wasn't coming, he should have called and let me know.

If there was anyone that could come up with a way to fix him, it was my girl.

Although she was married and settled down a little, she was more ready for some action. I think a year of marriage has just about stomped a mud hole in her spirit. She would call me at times telling me how Jr. Cefuss questioned her about everywhere she went. She said if she was in the restroom too long, he'd come, knock on the door, and ask if she was alright. She claimed he was driving her out of her mind, but whenever I was around them, I could tell she loved every minute of it.

I called Teeny Baby and explained everything that happened.

"I told you to call me when you wanted to talk, but no, you had to keep all of this a secret," was the first thing out of her mouth. "Beatrice, we could have taken care of this a year ago."

Teeny Baby started to tell me her plan and, boy, was it good. All I had to do was do my part to make it a success. Teeny Baby and Jr. Cefuss both belonged to Shady Creek Baptist Church. Teeny Baby was the secretary and Jr. Cefuss was on the deacon's board. Jr. Cefuss was becoming one of The Reverend Tavone's brightest and closest friends, when it came to church business, but off the court, Jr.'s love for Harry was untouchable.

Teeny Baby explained to Jr. Cefuss everything I had told her, not keeping anything out and Jr. Cefuss was furious. Teeny, instructed Jr. Cefuss to go to Reverend Tavone and tell him she was having an affair on him and that he would really appreciate if he gave a sermon on fornication. She told Jr. Cefuss to make sure to tell him that if the affair didn't stop, someone may get hurt. Jr. Cefuss was good at instructions because Teeny Baby has been telling him what to do way before they were married.

Teeny Baby said that Tavone told her if she ever needed to talk about anything, his door was always open. Everyone in town knew that Teeny Baby and I were good friends – except for Tavone. He lived in Virginia just to stay away from the, what he calls, trouble. Trouble followed him anyway.

Ma Elsie always said that God don't like ugly, and Tavone had gotten very ugly. What he didn't know was that I knew he had slept with Teeny Baby...And I knew Teeny Baby had fell in love with him. I knew she got pregnant by him and was going to have an abortion because he begged her to... telling her it would ruin him if anyone, including Trish, would ever find out. But Teeny Baby lost the baby before she was to go through with it. Teeny Baby tried to explain to me the when and why she fell for him. "I loved Harry and no one else, so I could not have cared less," I replied simply.

I freaked out when she first told me. I just remembered Beany telling me the story about the unborn baby she saw when Harry was living...damn she was seeing her family.

So much drama had been in my life right then that I needed a little something to settle me down. A little nourishment for the soul. This coming fourth Sunday would become fourth Sunday in the dirty, dirty South.

The bait that was set by Teeny Baby and Jr. Cefuss worked. There it was outside of the church in the middle of the church lawn. The information board read:

Quarterly meeting

March 24, 2002,
Fornication
Pastor T.P. McKnight.

Saturday night I was so excited I couldn't sleep a wink. On Sunday morning, I got the children up and dressed, and I took them over to Ma Elsie's house. Ma Elsie was going to Philadelphia Baptist Church of God and Christ. I wanted the kids to go with her because I didn't want them to experience fourth Sunday in the dirty, dirty South.

There Rev. McKnight stood in front of the congregation with a cream-colored double-breasted suit. His robe was a light blue color, which he left zipped down so everyone could see that his tie matched the burgundy floor shined shoes. The choir was singing the last hymn before it was time for Reverend McKnight to start his sermon. Trish was sitting over where the preacher's wife and the mothers of the church sat. The church was packed like sardines. By plan, I was to arrive last so that I could make an entrance. The signal for me to come in would be when Jr. Cefuss left the deacon's pew, went out the back door, and came around to give me the thumbs up. While I stood there waiting, I had another epiphany. I thought about everything Harry wrote in his letters. It came to me that all Harry ever wanted was to be a great father to Alex and Beany. Being that he knew he wasn't going to be here much longer, Harry wanted Tavone to be there for the children, not as a father, but someone to teach them and help them through life. Who could better take his place than Beany's real father? This was the day Tavone would either step up or step out.

Jr. Cefuss came around and gave me the thumbs up.
I waited for a minute to gather myself. Then, I walked in. Sitting in the congregation no particular order was Bucky, Teeny Baby, Lucy Gray, Knotts, and Lips. It was like my dream team for mayhem was front and center. As I walked down the aisle, I could see heads turning and people whispering. Mrs. Trish McKnight even looked at me like she could have kicked me like a tin can on the sidewalk.
Teeny Baby slid over so I could sit down. I looked at Tavone and he was looking as dumb as a doorknob.
He came up to the podium.
Teeny Baby was nudging me when it was time for me to stand up with my confession. Reverend McKnight started

reading from the New Testament.   We turned to *Corinthians Chapter 6, verse 9.*

"Raise your hands with a hallelujah to signal you're with me," the reverend said.

The congregation quickly raised hands in the air with a loud hallelujah.

"Follow me," the Reverend McKnight instructed to the congregation. **"Verse 9, *I wrote unto you in an epistle not to company with fornicators.   Verse 10, yet not altogether with the fornicators of this world, or with the covetous, or ex-covetous or with idolaters; For then ye needs go out of the world."***

It was time Teeny Baby elbowed me in the side.   I stood up.

"Yes, Mrs. Harold," Tavone said.

"God, I want to thank you for sending me my two children," I said.   "Rev, you know my little Alex and my sweet little Beany."

Reverend Tavone stood there like a deer froze in the headlights wondering when he should run.

"Well, they couldn't be here today."   Then I took a deep breath and said, "I had a child out of wedlock, and I prayed to God that He would give me the strength to raise her in righteousness."

By now, Teeny Baby was pulling on my dress for me to sit down, but I was like butter – I was on a roll.

"Lord knows I was wrong for having an affair and I ask for all ya'll to pray for me and my children.   My husband is gone and my daughter's real father, well, he tries to stay out of site."

Teeny Baby pulled on my dress once more, so I wiped the tears from my eyes and sat back down in my seat.   Tavone stood again for a moment wiping his face, stiff as a roach with the lights on staring at a can of Raid.

"We hear you, Sister Harold," said Tavone, "but right now," as his voice got louder, "I said, right now – y'all don't hear me! I said right now, preacher man's ready to preach!"

He started jumping around, whooping, and hollering, talking about fornication and how it was a sin.

Teeny Baby whispered in my ear.

"He's good, ain't he?"

"Yeah," I said, "he's good alright, but before we leave today, he's going to pay."

Teeny Baby must have thought of all the things he did to her and everything that had troubled her in her life because she jumped up in the middle of his sermon and said:

"Hold the flip up a minute, Mr. Preacher man. I have been sitting here listening to your snake in the grass ass self long enough. Ten years ago, you got me pregnant, and you said you were going to take care of your child, but you took care of it alright. You tried to pay for me to have an abortion…if I had not lost it first"

Before Teeny Baby could even finish, up stood two other ladies saying, "Yeah, you… no good heathen. You were probably going to spend the money for the building fund to pay for it."

Then another lady stood up and said:

"You're a sorry excuse for a man or human as far as I'm concern and all this time, I thought it was just you and me and your wife."

By this time, I was sitting there like Celie from the Color Purple waiting to see what color the walls were going to turn.

Trish stood up.

"Tavone, how could you?" Then Trish snatched the hat off Ms. Pearl and threw it at him.

133

Jr. Cefuss was so mad he just rushed to tackle the Reverend to the floor like Mean Joe Green. I guess he had no idea that Teeny Baby had been with Tavone. I guess Teeny Baby got carried away with all the excitement and told on herself.

Lips jumped up to help Jr. Cefuss kick Tavone's ass.

Knotts had his cell phone, calling the police for help, as Bucky stood there to hold back anyone trying to help Tavone. Trish got up, took the children, and hauled ass. I think she was just about as mad as a bull with a nosebleed. She stormed out the door, dragging the children behind her like she had a "Just married" sign written on her back and her children were the cans behind the car.

I looked outside and the sky was all purple there were people running everywhere...not really...back to the story...

When the smoke finally cleared, Tavone was lying at the pulpit in a pool of blood. I knew for sure he was dead. The police came, and the church was cleared out. The only people left was the people involved in the incident. No one wanted to end up in the *Daily Advancer*, the one newspaper that would inform you of everything going on in town, and this incident was definitely a front-page story.

Tavone wasn't dead by a long shot.

Lips took the blame for whipping Tavone's butt because he was so used of going in and out of jail. Lips figured he had nothing to lose compared to Jr. Cefuss. But Tavone didn't press any charges on anyone. Lips was released, so no harm, no foul was the verdict.

There it was, front page of the *Daily Advancer*, "Preacher Gets His Ass Kicked by his Congregation." Not really, it actually read, "Reverend Tavone McKnight Assaulted by Church Member." The story went into detail with the how, who, when, what, and why. And for those that didn't read the newspaper, Lucy Gray had them covered.

It was another porch day at Ma Elsie's to catch up on the weekly gossip. Ma Elsie said if she knew we were going to do this, she wouldn't have missed it for the world.

"Good for him," Ma Elsie said. "He made his bed, now it's time for him to sleep in it."

"Yeah," I said, "a soft ass makes a hard head."

Ma Elsie laughed.

"B.B., you got that just as ass backwards," she said, and we both died laughing.

Ma asked had I heard from Harry lately.

"No," I said, "I think Harry was pleased and is now at rest."

"Trish called me today and apologized for her actions and for Tavone's behavior."

"Did she leave him?" Ma Elsie asked.

"She said that God teaches you to forgive and that right now, she's probably going to just see what happens, but as of now, she's out. She was pretty nice and calm about everything, but I'm telling you if it would have been my Harry, if he wasn't dead, he would be by now."

Ma Elsie, sitting like a bantam rooster with that grin.

"Yeah baby, he sure would," she said.

I know she really meant, "Yeah – right."

I was enjoying Ma so much that I decided to spend the night. When I returned home the next day, my phone was blowing up with calls. That little red light was blinking like a traffic light. I hit the play button.

First, it was Teeny Baby telling me that she went to the jailhouse to sign for Lips' release. Then Lips called trying to leave a collect call. The next call was Lips and the next one and the next one, and then a message from Tavone asking for me to call back. I never returned Tavone's call, so he made a special trip over to the house. When his car pulled in the drive, I peeped out the window to make sure he wasn't carrying any kind of weapon on him. He rang the doorbell. Beany went to answer the door.

"Mom, it's Reverend McKnight at the door."

"Tell him to come in," I said. I was back in the bedroom cleaning up a little.

Although he made me sick, I still had to do the womanly thing. It's just in our blood to look our best when an old flame comes around. I walked in the living room and there he was, standing, holding Beany. I offered him a seat and told Beany to go in her room to play. Beany questioned why, and I slipped and said, "Your daddy and I have to talk."

"He ain't my daddy," Beany quickly replied, and walked into her room, stomping like she was in a marching band.

I turned to Tavone.

"So, what brings you to this neck of the woods?" Before he answered, I could tell by his eyes that whatever was on his mind was killing him inside.

"Beatrice," he said. "I'm sorry for all the troubles I caused, and if it was some way, I could take back the pain I've caused you, I would. But I can't. All I can do is start with today. I know all the answers to other people's problems, but not my own. So please tell me what to do."

Tavone was good, but he wasn't that good. I think he was starting to break down. His eyes were filling. One blink and the water was going to flow.

"Tavone," I said, "it's not all your fault. I had just as much to do with my situation as you did. The only problem I had is that you knew that Beany was your daughter all along and you never bothered to tell me. You let me go all through those years without knowing. Even though I didn't want to know, and I wanted her to be Harry's, you could have done the right thing and at least sent me a copy or something."

"Now, how was I supposed to send you a copy and you were married?" Tavone said.

"Well, you could have let me know some kind of way."

"How did you know that I knew all the time?" Tavone asked.

"Don't worry, I just knew," I said.

"So, where do we go from here?" Tavone said with a concerned demeanor.

"We? What do you mean we? Just do your part. Do what you can and what you think is right. You'll figure it out.

"Just trust the word, not the man in you."

137

CHAPTER 13
CLICKED ON THE SWITCH

For the last two years, it's like the devil has slipped something in my drink and screwed me. Although I was trying hard to push him off, he just kept pounding and thrusting himself on me. Not until I sobered up and shook him off did my path seem so clear to me. Each step I took made me stronger and each time I fell, I just dusted myself off and I befriended me even more.

It is like I never really knew who I was until I lost who I wasn't.

God has His ways of giving me all the power I need, it's just up to me to turn on the light, so I finally clicked on the switch.

Harry said that one day I would piece this whole thing together…and I have. He always warned me about Teeny Baby, and I never listened to him. Now, I understand that once you become partners for life in marriage, you must dedicate yourself to your long-term commitment of respecting and trusting each other. But I let Teeny Baby into the equation by trusting her a little too much. As a result, my marriage and my life were rocked. I wanted the best of both worlds when all I needed to be, was in Harry's world.

I am not taking the blame for his action. I'm only blaming myself for being so inconsiderate and so reckless with the vows we both made before God. I also understand that Harry was a man that really knew what love was because not too many men loved their family the way he did, knowing what he knew.

I just wish now I could have forgiven him the same way he forgave me.

Even in his death, he wanted only the best for his family. He wanted Tavone to step up to the plate and be there for Beany and Alex. I said Alex because if Harry took care of Beany, and he knew that she wasn't his, he expected for Tavone to take care of Alex. I think Harry couldn't understand he was an exception to the rule.

Even after the 4th Sunday in the dirty- dirty, Harry continued to visit Tavone until he was coming over almost every day doing stuff with Beany and Alex. Tavone had lost his wife through a nasty divorce and had joint custody with his children; I guess The Almighty told Trish to move on. Tavone would spend time a lot of days with his children and Beany and Alex. I often ask Beany does she ever see Harry, and she always answers, "No." I think Harry is sticking to the fact that Tavone was going to do his part, so he only visits Tavone when necessary. Tavone finally pieced his life back together. I think he now understands the meaning of serving one God – God almighty and not lust almighty.

He and I had already made peace, so moving on was all we had left to do.

The Reverend Tavone Mc Knight found another church in Virginia Beach near his home. He was a very gifted preacher. I know it had to have been his calling. Granted, he has blown a lot of smoke in his days and tried to burn the bridges he crossed, but he still spent a lot of time trying to help save lost souls, including his own, and turning the devil in to a liar. Tavone tells me that 4th Sunday in the dirty was the turning point in his life and I truly believe it was.

I guess you trust the Word and not the man unless you know the man. And does anyone really know anybody? I think not.

Now that the roles have reversed, I don't really bother Teeny Baby and Jr. Cefuss that much. The way I see it, she deserves to keep her marriage as honest as possible and if it called for me to distance myself, that would be her wedding gift from me. She always asks me to go with her and Jr. Cefuss to different outings, but I pretend that I have so much to do.

Maybe I'll just sit around and wait to see if another speeding turtle cross the road.

CHAPTER 14
ONE BIG PROMISE – DEATH

The March winds howled like the banshees.

I stood on the porch with Harry's old Duke Blue Devils jacket on, soaking in the breeze that will eventually bring in the summer heat. I reminisced about the days when I was a little girl running in the cornfields and trying to make my kite soar high into the clouds. Never thinking one day I would be looking up to those same skies, wondering when it would be my turn to soar like a kite to visit all the people I love so much.

Ma Elsie passed six months ago and now it's just the children and – me. Losing Ma Elsie made me understand that life came with one big promise – Death. And the way you feel when a new life comes into this world is met with an equal but opposite feeling when a life is taken. No matter how I had this all figured out, I some how managed to fall into this deep, deep depression. Running around in circles so fast that I allowed no one to catch me. I knew that Beany and Alex needed me more than ever now, but I was so selfish I could only focus on – me.

One day, Beany looked at me and started crying. I asked her what was wrong, and she pointed to my face. She said that I was starting to look like Ma Elsie when she was going to Heaven. I couldn't say anything; I just went into my bedroom and stared into the mirror. While looking into the mirror, I saw a reflection on the bed. The book *Black Frame* was lying there. I don't know how it got there, but there it was on the bed with a page folded. I opened the page and the poem "Early Grave" appeared as plain as day. It had been almost two years since I read anything from this book. It always seems like something, in this case someone, draws me to this book. I always felt like the poet had me in mind when he wrote this, so I began to read:

Early Grave

Am I smiling
Because…
I am blessed
Or
Am I
Blessed to have a smile
Understand…
My eyes are raining
So, I
Meditate for a while
Am I crying
Because…
I'm happy
Or
Am I happy
To be shedding tears
Understand
Right now
I'm happy
Because
I haven't rained
In years
Am I
Caught up in a cycle
Is there
A way I can be saved
Or

Should I just prepare
For
I'm headed to an early grave

I can't smell
Without the flowers
Yet
The odor is too sweet to smell
There are weeds
In my garden
Once upon I could not tell

I can't see
Without my mirrors
Because
They reflect the worse to be
Understand...
My eyes are raining
My light seems dark to me

Is there
Anyone who can help me
Should I
Help myself... be saved
Or
Am I a dead man walking
To an early grave

I no longer wanted to be a dead man walking, so I pulled myself together and went back into the living room and nourished the flowers God blessed me with and understood in time, the weeds in my life would eventually weed themselves out.

I believe Ma Elsie had something to do with that book being on the bed, with a little help from Beany, of course.

After Harry died, she used to always tell me that I was going to worry myself to an early grave and that I better find some way to dig myself out. "Don't worry, be happy," she used to say.

This year, I decided to reopen Harry's Sports Bar and Grill, but renamed it Harry and Son's Sports Bar and Grill. Alex was now 13 and Harry always promised Alex, when he was old enough, he would let him "run the bar." Alex was more than ready to start. I knew Bucky would be the first to show up, and he didn't let me down. What surprised me the most was Lips showing up to help also. I guess he felt like he owed me since the lawnmower incident.

While they were changing the garage into a sports bar, I had to leave and pick up Teeny Baby so we could head straight for Wal-Mart for supplies. This year was a little different because I was taking Beany with us for the first time. She was so excited that I wished I would have taken her all the other times. We even put her in charge of what type of drinks to get, being no alcohol would be served at the bar.

Time brings so much change. Teeny Baby and I didn't even get outfits like we used to. We would look and laugh, stirring up some old memories from the last sports bar parties. One reason Teeny Baby didn't buy anything was because she was eight months pregnant. I think she was feeling a little unpretty these days. I don't know what spread the most, Teeny Baby's nose or her ass. Every time I ask her, she answers with, "My breasts." With everything she and I have been through, good or bad, I just love her. I guess you can't get every weed out the flowerbed. All you can do is make sure it doesn't grow to large and always keep an eye on your flowers. I guess I'm just glad to be out with my best friend and my daughter.

The game started. Everyone was enjoying the food as well as the game. Teeny Baby and I still positioned ourselves so that we could laugh and talk about folks as they came in. What started it all was when Bucky brought that one loaf of bread. I guess some things never change.

Alex called me in to the kitchen.

"Mom." he said with the most beautiful smile on his face, "I pulled it off didn't I, Ma?" happy with his accomplishment. "I got all of my dad's friends here, didn't I?"

I smiled and was all teary eyed with my answer.

"You sure did, Alex. You sure did. Your daddy would be very proud of you."

"Yeah, he would be, wouldn't he?" said Alex.

I stood at the door leading to the garage looking at everyone as they enjoyed themselves and from back to front, and in no particular order were the flowers in my life's garden: Donald O'Neal Wilbert (Knotts), Michael Andre Jones (Bucky), Ella Sarah Cobb (Teeny Baby), Cleophus Joe Taylor, Jr. (Jr. Cefuss), Jeffery Daniel McDuffy (Lips), Harriet Elevese Harold (Hiddy), Alex Liman Harold, Breanna LaToya Harold (Beany), and Lucilla Victory Gray (Lucy Gray). There were a few others there, but they weren't invited, and they were weeds, as far as I knew. I finally understood the characters I made them all out to be were really people in their own strange ways, people who loved me and my family – even Lips, I mean, Jeffery.

It was half time and Alex said he wanted to do something different. He asked everyone to put all the chairs to the side. He then pointed to Beany to hit it. Beany hit the play button and the Electric Slide started to play on the CD player. Everyone started dancing. Even Teeny Baby tried to cut a rug. Suddenly, the music stopped. At first, everyone thought that a fuse had blown, but the TV was on, and it was plugged in the same socket. Then for some strange reason, Harry's eight-track tape started playing his favorite song in the shed. Soon, the song faded out as the CD player slowly faded back in. Then the doorbell rang.

Everyone was quiet, thinking that it was Harry returning from the dead.

"Go get my shotgun," I said.

Knotts stood looking like he had already seen a ghost.

On the count of three, we opened the door.

There he was standing looking all foolish in the face.

The Late Reverend Tavone McKnight…

He wasn't dead…yet… just late.

The End

About the Story

This story was inspired by the poems I have written throughout the story. This poem sums up the story.

The Word not The Man, an original poem by author and poet **Kent Hughes**. This poem, along with the others you have read in *4th Sunday in the dirty*, can be found in the book *Black Frame: Life inspired poetry* by **Kent Hughes.**

THE WORD AND NOT THE MAN

He stands in front of his congregation
Under his robe
He wore a suit tailor made
By his side
Sets a picture
Of
Ice cold… hand squeezed... lemonade
The choir had sung that song
You know the song they sang
before the preacher would preach
Rev kneels to say a prayer for strength
Now preacher man was ready to preach
He read a couple of scriptures from the New Testament
And the next words you would hear him say is...
I want to talk about fornication
That's my subject for today
But before he could utter another word
Up stood Sister Harold with the strangest look
on her face and said...
I'm glad you brought this subject up
at the right time and the right place
I have a child out of wedlock
He's sick and can't be here today
Rev, you know my little Alex

He's the one... that runs around church and praise
Now Lord knows I was wrong for having this affair
But I prayed and tried to raise him right
My husband left after the child was born
(The child was a little too dark skinned)
And the real father.... you know he tried to stay out sight
Sister Harold wiped the tears from her eyes
And soon sit back down in her seat
Rev said...
We hear you, Sister Harold...
but right now, preacher man ready to preach
Rev had the congregation saying Hallelujah
even Sister Harold said.... amen

Rev talked for about fornication and how it was a sin
Suddenly Sister Harold jumped up
yelling as loud as she could....
Just hold up a minute, Mr. Preacher man,
I've been sitting here listening
to this bullish_ t long enough
And I done stood all I could stand
Ten years ago, when you got me pregnant
You said that you were going to take care of your child
Well, you stared right at the boy and haven't even crack a smile
Rev, you know that boy is yours
The test came back positive... ninety-nine-point nine percent
And I haven't asked you for one single dime
And not one dime has you spent
Rev stood there sweating profusely
With his handkerchief in his hand
And said...
I never told you to trust in me
YOU TRUST THE WORD AND NOT THE MAN

About the author

Kent Hughes is a native of Camden, North Carolina. His hope is to inspire all, to follow him into a world where everything can be exactly the way you want it to be – if you capture your imagination and bind it in your own book.

BLACK FRAME

LIFE INSPIRED POETRY BY: KENT HUGHES

INTRODUCTON:

Writing poetry gives me a peace of mind that is food for the spirit. I decided to spoon-feed the reader with a little of what nourishes me. I have compiled a few of my favorites; some to inspire, some to encourage, and some to give all the vitamins needed to complete the frames in one's life.

I knew this task would have to be unique, entertaining, yet meaningful. I wanted everyone to feel as if I was writing with him or her in mind. I figured a good cry accompanied with a great laugh completes the soul. I decided to add some of my personality as a balance.

The first ingredient used to make this a success was writing on subjects that are heart moving, mind-bending, and soul-friendly (sometimes a remote control is used to change our minds, not the channel). I wrote three frames just in case you decided to change the channel: *LOVE AND RELATIONSHIPS, OUR CHILDREN, and SPIRIT/STRENGTH*. I also gave you a bonus entitled *MISFITS*, a few that did not fit in well with the others, but I'm sure you will feel them just the same.

The second ingredient was to write on subjects that in some way could inspire the reader to make a change or make a difference. Hopefully after you read **BLACK FRAME**, you will understand that we all go through the same frames, just at different times in our lives.

The two ingredients together were the birth of **BLACK FRAME.**

LOVE (RELATIONSHIPS)
OUR CHILDREN
SPIRIT (STRENGTH)
MISFITS (Bonus Frame)

"It's two things you don't do: step on my shoes or mess with my family."

Jesse Hughes, Sr.
(Father)

"Don't worry, be happy – and if that doesn't work, you'll have to ask someone greater than me."

Maiseville Hughes
(mother)

ACKNOWLEDGEMENTS

I am grateful to everyone who converged and provided me with time, space, confidence, and love needed to write this book.

To my co-worker: Yolanda Herring, thanks for the encouragement.

To Shelia: We did it, or didn't we? Whatever we did, it was your fault.

To Laura Sykes and Crystal Alexander: Thanks for your input.

To my co-workers: Thanks for the fill-ins.

To Kenesha Hughes: What can I say. You are 'the hostess'; I love you and thanks for listening.

To Theresa Figgs: I put your name in here. Now will you be my older sister again?

To my four sisters and two brothers: I love you all, especially Theresa Figgs (that's twice).

TABLE OF CONTENTS

FRAME TWO

MY   CHILDREN,   OUR
CHILDREN
MY   CHILDREN,   OUR
CHILDREN (SENERIO)

TOP OF MY LIFE
STAY ON MY MIND
IMAGE OF ME
TO LIVE FOR
YOUR CHILD
WHAT HAPPENED
JUVENILE INJUSTICE

FRAME THREE

SPIRITUALLY BASED
SPIRITUAL

I WOKE UP
WHERE I WANT TO BE
ALWAYS REMEMBER
GRACE AND MERCY
SAVE ME
REDEMPTION
PRAYER
A FRIEND
I LOVE YOU, MAN
TO BE WITHOUT
LIFE'S PLAY
TURN TO YOU

FRAME FOUR

MISFITS

THE WORD NOT THE MAN
THEY CALL-THEY WRITE-THEY COME
TO AN EARLY GRAVE
DARK LOVE
SHE
THE OLD MAN
BLACK FRAME GIRLFRIEND
AS LONG AS I
CHAIR OF DESPAIR
HE
VERDICT
THE NEXT TIME
JUST UNDERSTAND
CRACKS FROM THE STONE
SUNSHINE AND PRAYER
I PRAYED FOR THE CHILDREN
THE NEXT DAY
MOVING MY MOUNTAIN
BLEMISHED VISIONS
A CRY FOR HUMANITY
BLACK FRAME PROVERBS
FEELING ME

FRAME ONE

The Concept

KNOWING LOVE

THE GOOD, THE BAD, THE UGLY

I can speak only on what I have experienced or maybe what a friend shared. But, judging from the two, I have learned that love can be Good, Bad and Ugly; it all depends on how you treat love and how you allow love to treat you. Good relationships are something like spaceships: there have been a few sightings here or there, but do they really exist? Everyone seems to be searching for area 51, the area where only a few relationships work...so they say. It makes you wonder if how to love (and have a healthy relationship) is TOP SECRET.

Let's enter **BLACK FRAME** love and relationships.

The Good
The Bad
The Ugly

GOOD AS GOOD GETS
THE SCENERIO
PART 1

EVERY MOMENT...
Without you is time spent knowing
I truly need you forever.
Forever and...
EVEN LONGER...
I will show...
And tell you just how much you mean to me.
START TO FINISH...
Is the only way I know how to love you.
To make my day all I need is to...
GET A HUG FROM YOU...
Close my eyes and think of the time...
I HAD A DREAM...
About you.
Your...
BROWN FIRE...
Burns within me.
When you hold on to my...
LOVE HANDLES.
I know you will not...
TAKE MY LOVE...
For granted
Because you know my love is yours...
IF ASKED

THE GOOD

EVERY MOMENT

WITHOUT YOU

EVEN LONGER

START TO FINISH

GET A HUG FROM YOU

I HAD A DREAM

BROWN FIRE

LOVE HANDLES

TAKE MY LOVE

IF ASKED

EVERY MOMENT

With all the problems that we've
been through
    Our love has kept us blind
    And if we would meet on earth
ten times over
    I would choose you each of those
times.

    I know these are merely words
    They may not mean much to you
    But with every happy moment I
remember
    You were there to see me
through.

    Anytime I needed a believer
    You were by my side
    Whenever I needed a friend
    Your arms were open wide.

    You've given me more than I
could ask
    Yet asked for little in return
    The more you teach me about
your love
    The more eager am I to learn

LONGER

Before you understand the situation
You first must understand yourself

So, I tried to figure why I felt this way
Until emptiness was all that was left

I put myself in a position
That was uncomfortable for my heart

All lights were green and my tank half empty
Your love became my start

Your smile was my lover
Your kiss my closest friend

Your embrace was my comfort
Your eyes my undying end

For when I looked into your eyes
And didn't see the love we once felt

I smiled to hide the pain
But inside my heart just wept

So don't think I don't feel the same now
In fact, it has gotten even stronger

No matter what
I'll care forever
And love you even longer

START TO FINISH

We thought we had it all figured out
I understood you
You understood me
Everything seemed so beautiful on the
outside
We couldn't see the forest for the trees

It starts off with the small arguments
Which we never could get quite right
Then comes the part where you say
you hate me
By then it's the couch for the night

A few days pass we barely speak
Only saying words when necessary
We start acting nice
To break the ice
Cause for a minute it starts to get scary

The stage is set
For the grand finale
We are acting like we just met
We hug to make up for lost time
Maybe love's not done with us…yet

GET A HUG FROM YOU

If I followed a rainbow to the end
And found a pot of gold

I would still need you beside me
To have someone to hold

If I got everything I ever wanted
And all my dreams came true

I would not be satisfied
Until I got just one hug from you

If the stars in the heavens
Spelled out our name
If we made it in Heaven's greatest couple hall of
fame

All of that wouldn't mean a thing
If I couldn't get a hug from you

I HAD A DREAM

I had a dream I was being touched
In a way that felt so real
My body was in a state of shock
Her hands were truly skilled

With each embrace
She encircled me softly
But oh, so tight
I had a dream
A beautiful dream
I wish had never ended that night

Falling deeper into a hypnotic state
She appeared to me once more
Traction exerted on my back with her hands
Felt better than ever before

A light stroke of her tenderness
Put me in a heavenly peace-like trance
My body was confused from what I was going
through
And she understood my circumstance
So….
She let me down softly
When she got off me
Leaving me craving for her touch
I had a dream
A beautiful dream…damn I dream too much

BROWN FIRE

Hot to the touch
Smooth for the eyes
A deep pleasure for the mind

A dream for dreamers
A wish for wishers
An absolute soul divine

Stay on not off me
Tell me I'm your desire

But burn me not
Because I think you're hot
My sweet irresistible brown fire

Love me tender
Love me long
Tie my heart in a knot

Your sex is sexy
If you need love
I'd say next...me

Damn it's getting hot

The blood starts boiling
The sweat starts pouring
My body is for your hire

But burn me not
I think you're hot
My sweet irresistible brown fire

169

For your love I would wait
Wouldn't hesitate
I would be there awaiting the flame

I would keep driving you wild
Not deviating to mild
Until you should call out my name

Your love is so hot it replaces my sun
I need your love
More than anyone

You are the one
I admire

But burn me not
I think you're hot
My sweet irresistible brown fire

LOVE HANDLES

Turn down the lights my love
Put the locks on the doors
You pour just a little bit of wine
I'll slide the mattress to the floor

Tonight, and all night I'm
making you happy

You said you've never been in
love
Well, I've been there a time or
two
But tonight, let's forget about our
past
I want to concentrate on you

Grab my love handles and let me
take you for a ride

You can be on bottom for a while
Then work your way on top
Once we get this love thing going
I can't promise you I will stop

Tonight, and all night I'm
making you happy

They say that love don't love
anyone
I don't believe that's true
Because I have so much love
inside

171

And I want to share it all with
you

Grab my love handles and let me
take you for a ride

The night has caught us creeping
Embracing each other tight
I can't believe I shared my love
with you
With you holding my handles so
tight

Tonight, and all night, I am
making you happy

TAKE MY LOVE

Take my love…keep it warm

Place it gently in your pocket

Take my heart…
keep it safe

Place it in a box and lock it

Take my mind…
teach it to love

Leave me with so much to say

Take my body…
you know it's yours

Because you take my breath away

IF ASKED

If asked…
to describe my love

If asked…
how far I'd take my love

Forever is how far I would go

If asked…
how do I love thee

I could not count the ways

I'd just wish and hope for a better love
And pray for better days

And if for some reason God should take us
Far away from here
I'd wait to find my place in Heaven
Because I know I'd find you there

If asked...

BAD BLOOD BOILING
THE SCENERIO
PART 2

LOVE IS MY NEMESIS and
When I questioned love, its only reply was…
I THOUGHT YOU KNEW.

WHAT THEY REALLY WANT…
I couldn't begin to tell you because it seems like
THE MORE I TRY…
The more love beats me down.
One thing about love is
WHAT COMES AROUND GOES AROUND.
Seems like love has no weight, space, or time when it's good
But there is a thickness that weighs the heart when love goes bad
But…
MAYBE THAT'S JUST ME…
And maybe that's why the
THREE TEARS…
Falling from my eyes give me
ONE GOOD REASON…
To keep loving forever

THE BAD

LOVE IS MY NEMESIS
I THOUGHT YOU KNEW
WHAT THEY REALLY WANT

175

> *THE MORE I TRY*
> *WHAT   COMES   AROUND*
> *GOES AROUND*
> *MAYBE THAT'S JUST ME*
> *THREE TEARS*
> *ONE GOOD REASON*

LOVE IS MY NEMESIS

I've battled love for many years
And I've lost almost every war

But what did I do that for

Love whispered softly in my ear
And had me in a delusional state
Then like a hot dinner prepared before me

Love served my heart on a plate

I trusted love would fulfill me
But I craved for more than a bite
I tasted the best love had to offer

Then I lost my appetite

Until love touched my weakest spot
And had me melting like ice cream in the sun
Then love explained to me with anticipation

How it was just trying to have fun

So, I stared love straight in the eyes
And love gave me the sweetest smile
So, I followed love as it led the way

Love said it liked my style

Love led me straight to misery and pain
Sometimes I wish love would cease to exist
I guess I'm just a sucker for love

For love is my Nemesis

177

I THOUGHT YOU KNEW

I must have...
                    sang every
love song

I must have...
                    said every
prayer

Looking for love...
                    after love
lost me

Just to find no love
there

It hurts when...
                    you love
someone

And for some reason...
they won't love you
back

You put your heart into
their every word
And every word turns
your heart black

Question?

Was it something I said?

or
Was it something I did?

To keep you away from
me

Was the money not
enough?
Did I run when times
got rough?
Will you please tell me
what to do?

And stop saying I
thought you knew.

WHAT THEY REALLY WANT

I hear it all the time from the ladies
That a good man is hard to find
I think what they want is
Someone that can read their minds

Someone that knows when they want to be touched
And when they want to be left alone
Someone to…
wash the clothes

clean the house
and be at work

Before they get home

Someone to praise them like they're goddesses
And bow to their every need
And if you get half of what they want correct
Then just maybe you have done a good deed

I hear it all the time from the ladies
That a good man should be ready and willing
I think what they really want is
Someone that really understands their feelings

Someone to stay when they tell them to leave
Someone to leave when they tell them to stay
Someone to say…
Yes honey
I'll get it honey

You're right honey
I'll fix it honey

And she will sarcastically say "today"

If your relationship happens to work
Look up at space and thank the stars

Women are from Venus and men are from
their MOTHERS

THE MORE

The more I try…
to love you
The less you seem to care

The more I want…
you in my life
The less you want to be there

I try to pretend that I'm ok
And that everything is fine
But you zero in on my emotions
Just like you're reading my mind

The more I try…
to hurt you
The more I hurt myself

The more I need…
you to listen
The more you seem to go deaf

I can't go on like this
Feeling like I feel
You know the routine

Call me…

When you want a love that's real

COMES AROUND GOES
AROUND

There is no need in talking
There is nothing left to say
I tried to show you a good love
But you did not want to love this way

Time after time my arms were open
wide
And you passed right through
You said that I wasn't enough of what
you need
And that I was just something to do

Why call me when you're lonely
It's not healthy to play with my mind
You know I'm a fool for a lonely heart
Why call me...if I'm not your kind

I feel right now that I have no choice
So, I'll stay and keep playing your
game
But you can best believe
What comes around goes around
And one day you will be treated the
same

183

MAYBE THAT'S JUST ME

Do you even care about what I'm
feeling?
Do you care at all I ask?
Why can't you see the pain?
That hides behind the mask

How can you be so thoughtless?
Do you think about me at all?
I remember it all so clearly
When once you had a fall

Can a person be self-righteous?
How self-righteous can one
person be?

I personally think it's low self-
esteem
But maybe that's just me

Well, I guess your heart beats for
life only
And my heart beats for life and
love
When I think about you and the
whole ordeal

What was I really thinking of?

THREE TEARS

I made mistakes played silly
games
Cashed my heart in to pay for my
wrongs
I would leave in the middle of
the night
Without saying I'm gone

You cried and tried to reach out
for me
I would turn my back and walk
away
You asked what my problem was
And not one word would I say

But if there's anything I can do
To pay for what I've done
I would climb to the top of the
world
Just to claim you my number one

I guess for now
You can count three tears of this
clown

My friends used to tell me
How I didn't treat my lady right
And if they had someone like
you
With a heart that's true
They would hug and squeeze you
tight

185

But you know I'm like any man
I didn't pay them any mind
Now I sit in this lonely home
Because you left me behind

But if there's anything I can do
To pay for what I've done
I would climb to the top of the world
Just to claim you my number one

I guess for now
You can count three tears of this clown

ONE GOOD REASON

Give me one good reason…
To walk away
And you will probably make me
run

Give me one good reason…
I shouldn't stay
Because I can't think of
none

Tell me why …
You hurt so much
Please don't say it's me

Because just like you, I'm
tired too
So, for once…
Can we let this be?

THE UGLY STORY
THE SCENARIO
PART 3

I know I've got problems
Because…
YOU'VE GOT PROBLEMS…
And our problem is…
THE OTHER WOMAN'S ON YOUR MIND.
Even when we are …
TRYING…

It never seems to work out…

All I wanted was for us to…
Sit down and talk…
ONE NIGHT THIS WEEK
To work out our problems…

It's too bad that our dreams of being together…
Forever…
Only lasts for…
SEVEN YEARS.

THE UGLY

**YOU'VE GOT PROBLEMS
THE OTHER WOMAN'S ON
YOUR MIND
TRYING**

ONE NIGHT THIS WEEK
SEVEN YEARS

YOU'VE GOT PROBLEMS

You know you've got problems
When you'd rather be at work
than at home

You know you've got problems
When your spouse is butt naked
And you'd rather have the T.V.
on

You know you've got problems
When you can't get a simple
hello
From your spouse

You know you've got problems
When the children are controlling
The whole damned house

You know you've got problems
When your voice just makes your
spouse feel sick

You know you've got problems
When your spouse learns
A new lovemaking tricks

KENT HUGHES

You know you've got problems
When your spouse says
It doesn't feel the same

        And you know you've got
problems
        When your spouse is asleep
        And calls out someone else's
name

THE OTHER WOMAN'S
ON YOUR MIND

You speak of her like you want her
Seems you talk about her everyday
She's in your head like a demon
All the while I wish her away

You   compare   when   there's   no
comparing
Why do you give her so much life?
You even let her mess up our groove
Maybe she should have been your wife

You ask about things from my past
Then you act like it was yesterday
This is our life we bought into
Why do you insist she play

You give her so much power
Boy! Only if she knew
Why keep bringing her name up
Damn!
Glad she doesn't have a clue

You almost act like you love her
If you do, I won't be mad
It's almost twelve midnight
Let's finish the conversation in bed

Good Night!

TRYING

I'm sitting here trying to figure out
Why we keep falling apart
Wanting to understand your tears
But I don't know where to start

One-minute things are going great
The next a frown's on your face
They say misery loves company
I think misery lives at your place

How long do we go through this
The time is in your hands
I have tried to make you feel like a
woman
So, for once make me feel like a man

Try putting yourself in my position
Think about when we made that step
The promises you wanted me to keep
Are the same ones you haven't kept

Tonight, when you say your prayers
Say a sincere one for us both
Because if we don't come together as
one
It's the children who suffer most

ONE NIGHT THIS WEEK

So, you stayed out late last night
Thinking you are single and free
What about promise and commitment
Those words sound familiar to me

When we wanted a child
God gave us a child
Then you shifted in another direction
Now you complain about us spending
time
And how I don't show you any
affection

The pain and problems that you have
caused
I can only come to one conclusion
Since you are always part of the
problem
Then you, leaving must be the solution

193

SEVEN YEARS

I don't want to give up

Because I have too much at stake
But I'm losing bits and pieces of
myself
Until now it's whatever it takes
I have exhausted all my emotions
And I've cried my very last tear
It's too bad that our forever
Only last for seven years

The problems are complicated
The solution is simple
Communication would overturn the
hatred
But we can't talk without losing our
temper

I'm tired of listening to how much you
hate me
It's starting to pollute my ears

Too bad that our forever
Only last for seven years

The vows we made to each other
Were promises I wanted to keep
But with all the pain I've been through
I wish I were talking in my sleep

I would have been gone by now
But with freedom also comes fear

It's too bad that our forever

4th SUNDAY
Only last for seven years

FRAME   TWO

The Blueprint

MY CHILDREN, OUR CHILDREN

I've never understood how any two people could have a child and choose to be irresponsible. Yes, being irresponsible is a choice. Nor could I understand a mother or father getting so caught up in his or her own dysfunctions that they ignore a child's life, which is at stake.

I am a father of three girls, and I choose to be responsible. I'm always reminded that they didn't choose to be here, I made that choice...kinds...LOL. What is a good father? Is it just sending the check or checking yourself? Is it just spending money on birthdays or spending time? Or both...

Yes, the children are our future. But at this point, that phrase brings a sense of melancholy. If our present doesn't change, our future will not be too promising. I say this because we are leaving too many children behind. The children that make it seem to be slowly torn down by the children that do not.

With the few words that have been said that carry so much weight, here is the **BLACK FRAME** of mind.

THE CHILDREN, THE CHILD
THE PRAYERS
> When I stand at the
>> *TOP OF MY LIFE...*
>> I reflect on what means the world
to me.
> I first think of my children.
>> Kenesha,
>>> Chasity
>>> And
>>>> Tamaia
>> They have me helped reach the top...

> They constantly...
>> *STAY   ON   MY*

MIND...
> Because they are all an...
>> *IMAGE OF ME.*
> My children are simply...

>> *TO LIVE FOR.*
> God I am...

>> *YOUR CHILD...*
> And like the flowers in your garden, you
nourished me and watched me blossom into a responsible
adult...
>> Now the questions remain...
>> *WHAT   HAPPENED   TO   THE*
CHILDREN
> And are they victims of our
>> *JUVENILE*

INJUSTICE

> OUR CHILDREN

TOP OF MY LIFE
STAY ON MY MIND

199

KENT HUGHES

IMAGE OF ME
TO LIVE FOR
YOUR CHILD
WHAT HAPPENED TO THE CHILDREN?
JUVENILE INJUSTICE

THE TOP OF MY LIFE

I climbed to the top of my life

To look back at what I had learned

To look back on what I had learne   I found that

the flames inside me

As a child had never ceased to burn

I saw the drummers beating their drums

As I went toward the sound

I followed the footsteps of my forefathers

Their sweat and blood helped pave the ground

For me to walk upon the ground

I crawled before I would stand

Even when I thought I was ready

I wasn't close to being a man

KENT HUGHES
An elder told me

About the path he had to cross

Even as a child I understood

How he helped pay the cost

I saw myself in my teenage years

I was infinity at the time

Until I saw my friends pass before me

And soon had a change of mind

Although I struggled through my teenage years
I made it from a boy to a man

I saw myself being impatient
But later I would understand

I then climbed down from the top of my life
To look forward to what I can learn

And remember that the flames   inside me as a
child
Were always meant to burn

STAY ON MY MIND
A FRAME FOR KENESHA

It's been so long since I've seen you
You stay on my mind
Sorry that I'm so far away
I remember the day when you were born
I remember your first cry
Now look at you
You're all grown up
It's funny how time passes by

Only you need to know I love you;
you know I always will
Sometimes I close my eyes
You are all I see and feel
The road has kept our distance

But you will always stay in my heart

Every chance I have I'll spend with you
Even death can't keep us apart

IMAGE OF ME

A FRAME FOR CHASITY

Are you going to work to play with your friends?
Daddy, I want to go with you and soon after, the
crying begins

I leave out on a thirty-minute commute
Thinking about what she just said
Knowing what I was facing at work
I almost wish I had
Taken her with me that day
Knowing my face would have kept a smile

It's funny how you can see images of yourself
In the eyes of your child
I made it through work that day
But couldn't wait to get back home
When I got there, she ran and jumped on me
You would have thought she was there alone

I can't imagine how I would exist
Or just where I would be
But I sure thank God and the Heaven above
For sending her down to me

TO LIVE FOR
A FRAME FOR TAMAIA

I lived for myself for so many years

My life became an art

Never did I imagine a part of me

Taking control of my heart

Along came this little angel

I was reevaluating my life again

The one creation that's a part of me

The beginning of my someday end

I speak of you my little one

In which my life, I wouldn't hesitate to give

For without someone to die for

You can't really say you've ever lived

YOUR   CHILD

Help me to be strong
Inspire, encourage, and honor my thoughts
Push me forward when I fall behind
Pick me up when I'm down
Be my strength when I'm weak
My voice when I can't speak
Direct me when I'm lost
Show me how to, even when I think I know
Teach me when I want to learn
Teach me even more when I don't
Love and protect me forever

Because after all I am...
YOUR CHILD

WHAT HAPPENED

What happened
To the children
Why do they
Make us cry
Why do they
Allow one teardrop
To fall from their mother's eye?

What happened
To our fathers'
Why did they
Run away
What are they
Really thinking and
What would their father's say?

When will
We stop the madness
Who answers
When God calls
When time finally runs out?

Will Heaven help us all?

JUVENILE INJUSTICE

Unfairness, pleads the innocent
It's not fair. pleads the child
Guilty before innocent
I know you think I am,

But it's not my fault
I'm like this
You see my mom
She just doesn't care
My father…
Don't even ask
You know damned well he's not there.

Judge, if you adjudicate me
You'll probably see me again
Juvenile injustice starts at home
At home is where it begins.

I'll try to explain it to you, judge,
Since you're letting me have my say
Ever since I was a toddler
My mom always let me have things my

way

She told me that no child of mine
Would ever want for anything
So, I grew up thinking the world owed

me

And I wanted everything
If someone tried to correct me
When I was doing wrong
My mom would step right in
And tell them, "Leave my baby alone"

That let me know right then and there
That I could get away with my actions
Because my mom would always take
care
Of all my major infractions

My father drank and smoked that stuff
When he came around, he was always high
The only advice he gave
Was that a man is not supposed to cry

So, I held back my tears

Smoked and drank like my father
And claimed to be a man
So, your, Honor, it can't be my fault
You've got to understand

Judge, if you adjudicate me
You'll probably see me again
Juvenile injustice starts in the home
At home is where it begins.

FRAME

THREE

The
Construction

SPIRITUALLY BASED

God has given me strength. The test of strength comes from encounters during a lifetime. To have strength to endure any circumstance, I had to connect with my spirit. Allowing my spirit to guide me was my first true ambition. I now know not only about life, but how life should be lived.

In touch with the spirit...**THE BLACK FRAME** way.

THE
STRENGTH,
THE SPIRIT
THE BLESSING

I WOKE UP...
This morning and realized that I'm just
WHERE I WANT TO BE.
I will
ALWAYS REMEMBER...
How blessed I am when I think of God's...
GRACE AND MERCY,
Which will...
SAVE ME...
From life's sometimes sorrowful plays.
REDEMPTION...
And daily
PRAYER...
Has brought me through life's struggles.

Being that...
God is...
A FRIEND
He never hesitates to tell me...
I LOVE YOU, MAN
And...
TO BE WITHOUT...
God's love would be the end of...
MY LIFE'S PLAY
And like the beginning of the end...

4th SUNDAY
I would again…
TURN TO YOU.

SPIRITUALLY BASED

I WOKE UP
WHERE I WANT TO BE
    ALWAYS REMEMBER
    GRACE AND MERCY
    SAVE ME
    REDEMPTION
    PRAYER
    A FRIEND
    I LOVE YOU, MAN
    TO BE WITHOUT
    LIFE'S PLAY
     TURN TO YOU

I WOKE UP

I woke up this morning
Wondering how I was going
to make it through the day
I had given up
Before barely getting out of
bed

Saying my prayers
Before placing my feet gently
to the floor
I realized my battle was
already won
*When **I woke up** early this
morning*

WHERE I WANT TO BE

Tired of fighting my way through life
Needing my derailed journey placed on track
And whenever I look forward to tomorrow
Yesterday starts holding me back
Procrastination has played its part
To keep me in my place
My destination is painted in my dreams
The passage written on my face

I have all that I'm obligated to have
Yet I yearn for so much more
My attitude reflects my obsession
My destination the brightest door
No more walking through life with blinders on
Pretending that I can't see
I'll keep pushing forward
Taking quantum leaps
Until I'm where I want to be

ALWAYS REMEMBER

Remember to appreciate family
And always honor a true friend
Be thankful and humble to those
who help you
From beginning to end

Always love thy neighbor
As you should love yourself
Believe in your wildest dreams
And worry about nothing else

Never say you can't do it
Always give it a try
Before you decide to give up
Always question yourself… why?

If you remember nothing else
Remember what a friend told me
In life, never let anyone…
Rent a space in your head for free

GRACE AND MERCY

That shows GOD'S mercy and grace

You can see it on a passer-by
By the smile on their face

You feel it in the morning
When the sun reels its shinny head

You see it in the nighttime
The moonlights on your bed

You see it when the rain falls
Softly to the ground

They're signs of GOD'S grace and mercy
Just take a look around

SAVE ME

I will not cry anymore
For HE has opened my door
Now all I must do
Is walk through and believe
For HE said it would be alright
So, before I go to bed tonight

I'll fall on my knees
Ask the LORD
To help me take that first step

Because my GOD said
HE would

And my GOD said
HE could

Most of all
I know HE will… save me

REDEMPTION

Redemption; regain, free, or resave by paying a price
Atone for; free from sin; convert into something of value.

To regain one's freedom one must think freedom
Free of mind, free of body and free of soul
Of these a price must be paid.

THE COST of REDEMPTION
condition yourself

Forget-what has passed you by and start your
resurrection.

Atonement- make amends with those (friend and foe)
A whole man is not measured by his weight,
but by the context of his character.

Remember-your sins, understand what they are
and their results.
But never forget your spirit, which is your life given force.

Convert into someone you can live with
only then will the dying stop.

And always remember that growth doesn't come with height, but with understanding and wisdom.

KENT HUGHES

PRAYER

If ever a day I awake
And my sun doesn't seem to shine
That's the day I'll keep on praying
To keep this light of mine

The simple ways in life sometimes
Confuses mankind all day
But the more I keep in touch with God
The more He leads the way

A FRIEND

I know a FRIEND I can call my own
I know someone who loves me
When the love seems gone
I call HIS name
And through the magic of belief
He saves my soul
Makes me whole
And washes away my grief

In my life
I've had my ups
Trust me.... I've had my downs
But never
Have my feet
Hit rock bottom ground

See my GOD said
If you take one step, HE will take two
I believe in the FATHER
I believe in the SON
Like THEY believe in you

I LOVE YOU, MAN

Piece me together, father
I'm starting to fall apart
I'm holding on by faith
I've trusted you from the start

Mold me in the image
Of the strongest man on earth
Teach me the wisdom and understanding
That you taught me since my birth

Embrace me with your loyalty
That has kept me here thus far
Point me in the right direction
Show me your brightest star

Sit me down just one more time
Only like you can
For you are my first hero
And, Dad, I love you man

Piece me together, father
I didn't know the world was so cold
I've tried to do things my way
But my way is getting old

Pour some life back in me
So that I may breathe once more
This time I'll listen to that long talk
Wish I had listened before

Show me how to fix my woes
And how to hold my head up high

Tell me again how I'm a man and how it's okay to cry

No matter how I walk through life

I'll always hold your hand

And never forget what you have done for me

Because, *Dad, I love you man*

TO BE WITHOUT

To fly without wings

Is to dream

To love without preparation
And to care without condition

Is to be blessed

To find without looking
And to seek without answers

Is to be patient

To have without wanting
And to request without needing

Is to be thankful

To be with
        or
 To be without

Is to live…
To be…

And to dream

LIFE'S PLAY

I'm known for being in control of
my direction
Taking the lead part in the play
of my life
Never getting emotional, I'm
exceptional
With a mind as sharp as a knife

Always challenging the storms
with protection
Knowing the clouds can't rain
me down
I love me so I show me affection
I'm programmed to when no
one's around

My strength comes from so many
places
My cries are buried deep inside
My faith battles the monsters of
my many faces
And hope reaches out with arms
open wide

I hold myself responsible for my
happiness
Anticipating and appreciating
each day
I will search for peace nothing
more nothing less
And let GOD be the critic of my
play

TURN TO YOU

When I can no longer feel the
wind
Dancing on my face
When tomorrow skips me by
And I no longer know my place
That's when I will turn to you
And ask you for that missing time
So, I might have the strength
To leave yesterday behind

When I can no longer feel the sun
Massaging my back
When tomorrow I see my future
And it's slipped through the cracks
That's when I will turn to you
And ask you for your hand
So that I might have the wisdom
To one day understand one day

When I no longer feel the rain
Falling softly on my skin
That's when I will turn to you
And beg you to let me in
And when I no longer take that
breath
That you gave me at my birth
I would have already turned to you
To release me from this earth

FRAME FOUR

The building

MISFITS

I had written a few poems and short stories that just didn't seem to fit into any Frame. So instead of omitting them, I decided to list them at the end of the book and use the appropriate title, MISFITS.

I found them to be interesting, but somewhat strange ... you know the BLACK FRAME way. Let's wonder into the island of the misfits.

THE WORD NOT THE MAN

He stands in front of the congregation
Under his robe he wore a suit tailor-
made
He has his sermon all written up in his
head

And by his side…a glass…of…
Ice cold
Hand squeezed
Lemonade

The church choir had sung that song
You know the song they sing
before the preacher would preach

Rev knelt to say a prayer for strength

Now preacher man was ready to preach

He started quoting scriptures from the
New Testament
Soon after you could hear him say
"I want to talk about fornication
That's my subject for today."

But before he uttered another word

Up stood Sister Harold…

With the strangest look on her face

She said, "I'm glad you brought this
subject up

231

At the right time and the right place
You see I have a child out of wedlock
He's sick and can't be here today
Rev, you remember my little Alex
He's the one that runs around church
and plays

I know it was wrong for me to have an
affair
But I prayed and tried to raise him right
My husband left soon after the child
was born
And the real father tried to stay out of
sight."

Then Sister Harold wiped the tears
from her eyes
As she sat down in her seat

The Rev said, "We hear you,
Sister Harold.

Now preacher man is ready to
preach."

He had the congregation
Crying Hallelujah…
A couple of Yesss, Jesus'!…
Even Sister Harold said, "Amen"

The Rev preached on for about
an hour on fornication…
And how it was a sin

All of sudden
Sister Harold jumped up…

And yelled from the top of her lungs

"Hold up a minute, Mr. Preacher man:
I've been listening to you for about an hour
And I have stood all I can stand
Ten years ago
When you got me pregnant
You said, "I will take care of my child."
Well, you have seen him every Sunday for ten years
And you haven't even cracked a smile
Rev, you know that my boy is yours
The test was positive ninety-nine-point nine percent
I haven't asked you for even one single dime
And not one dime have you spent."

As he stood sweating profusely
With the handkerchief in his hand
Rev said, "I never told you to trust in me
YOU TRUST THE WORD, NOT THE MAN

THEY CALL
THEY   WRITE-
THEY COME

THEY CALL ME AT WORK…
Wondering when I can pay
I tell them the check is in the
mail
The same as yesterday

THEY CALL ME AT HOME…
The answering machine picks up
They leave a number for me to
call back
And once again they're out of
luck

THEY WRITE TO MY JOB…
Telling my boss, I'm deep in
debt
He borrowed five dollars from
me
That's why I'm not fired…yet

THEY   WRITE   ME   AT
HOME…
Explaining that my credit's going
bad
If they could check my credit
They would damned sure be mad

THEY COME TO MY JOB…
Trying to repossess my car
With the transmission gone
And the engine light on
They won't get very far

234

THEY COME TO MY HOME…
Trying to take my washer and dryer
I explained to them that I paid the bill
They are turning me into a liar

ONE DAY WHEN I GET CAUGHT UP…
I'll put all of them to shame
I'll put everything I ever owned
In my mama's name.

TO AN EARLY GRAVE

Am I smiling because I'm blessed
Or am I blessed to have a smile
Understand my eyes are raining
So, I... meditate.... for a while

Am I crying because I'm happy
Or am I happy to be shedding tears
Understanding that I'm happy
Because I have not rained in years

Am I caught up in a cycle
Is there anyway I can be saved
Or should I just keep sending myself
TO AN EARLY GRAVE

Can I smell without the flowers
Or is the odor too sweet to smell
There are weeds in my garden
Once upon I could not tell

I can't see without the mirrors
But they reflect the worse...to be
Understand my eyes are raining
My light is dark to me

Is there anyway I can be helped
Can I help myself.... Get saved?
Or am I a dead man walking
TO AN EARLY G RAVE

DARK LOVE

My rainbows are in black and
white
My blue skies are gray
I swear I see demons
Right before I pray
Every time I move a step forward
I fall two steps behind
If I can't have you
I'm going to lose my mind

I need you girl in my life

My tears they fall from my eyes
They are dry like sand
Sometimes I want to take my life
With my very own hands

The dawn brings new darkness
In the day the moonlight shines
If I can't have you
I'm going to lose my mind

I need you girl in my life

237

SHE

She hardly comes out of her
room these days
Rarely does she speak or smile
The problem started at the age of
sixteen
When she decided to have child

She watched as her mother
struggled
With two jobs to make ends meet

She figured since no time was
spent with her
She'd have a child
"Someone to love me for me."

She ignored all the warning signs
Even her friends told her
She was going about this wrong

She simply said, "It's my body
It will be my child
So just leave me the hell alone."

As naïve as her friends told her
she was...

She has an obsession with a plan
Love my child
Unconditionally...
Get help from the government...
And leave the rest in God's
hands

She started searching for the prefect candidates
Someone respectful…
Handsome…
And smart

But soon settled for any thug that would have her
Disregarding her head and heart

The mother…

You ask?

Where was the mother?

Why didn't mom step in?

My guess is…

Mom was busy working two jobs
And trying to be a friend

Well…

The truth is…
She found herself…
Lonelier…
Way lonelier…
Then before…

And because of all the wrong guys she chose
She found love wasn't love anymore

You see...

She's been going through a lot
these days
And it's been going on for quite
a while

Imagine...
This has everything to do with a
bad decision
Nothing to do with a child

She   contacted   the   AIDS
VIRUS...
Before she was seventeen...
And continued to have sex.
Because she did not know

Now she knows and...

She told me to tell anyone that
would listen
To...
Practice abstinence...
Safe sex
If you must

And remember...
SHE told you so...

She hardly comes out of the
room these days
Rarely does she speak or smile
Her problems all started at the age of sixteen
When she decided to have a child

THE OLD MAN

The old man sits by the window
The young man sits in his cell
The old man...prepares for Heaven
The young man...is living in Hell

They both sing songs...of forgiveness
They both cry tears...of regret
The old man tries...to remember
The young man tries...to forget

One anticipates the sun each morning
And for the other...it's one day at a time
The old man...thanks God for his sanity
The young man...is losing his mind

They both...have skeletons in their closets
They both know...one thing is clear
The old man...didn't do his part
And the young man...didn't ask to be here

The old man sits by the window
Watching the apples... fall not far from the tree

If the old man had picked up one apple (his own)

Then just maybe…the young man

would have been…free

BLACK FRAME AND GIRL FRIEND

BLACK Talk to me my sister
FRAME: Tell me what's on your mind
First tell me why he's hitting you
And why is it the same old line?

Telling me how he's a good provider
And a great father to the kids

Let me hear how he takes care of you
Just like your father did

Tell me again how he's stressed out,
that you nag him too much sometimes
And I'll tell you how he's full of it
And that you must be losing your mind

No human deserves that kind of treatment
Hell, dogs get treated better than that
By the way he's fifty pounds overweight
Why is he calling you fat?

Keep thinking you owe him something

Keep being his punching bag

I've seen the same situation before

Where the poor lady ended up dead

GIRL   If you stop talking for a minute

FRIEND: You can hear my side of the story

First of all, he only hit me twice

So, if I was you, I wouldn't be worried

And yes, my man is a provider

And a great father to our kids

He brought me a ring after an argument

And that's not half of what he did

He even took me to the movies

After he pushed me to the floor

And since I lost a few pounds

He hardly calls me fat anymore

Now let me get off this phone

And take your number off the caller ID

As a matter of fact, don't call for a while

I don't want that man killing me

BLACK   Okay, talk to you later

FRAME:

AS LONG AS I

As long as I accept the knife in
my back
You will continue to take stabs at
me

As long as I let your words build
my bridges
You will continue to tear down
my way across

As long as I live for you
You will let me die

But when I decided
I had enough
You placed down the knife of
hurt
And took a stab at kindness

You found that kind words-built
trust
And I began to crossover the
bridge to me
Now I believe in myself
Now I will let me…
Live

CHAIR OF DESPAIR

I placed…
A chair of despair
Into the dark corners…
Of my mind
I sat and stared into…
            This little light
That I once…
            Could never find

The light projected…
            My life stories
And the mistakes…

            From my yesterdays
I studied the light…
            To understand
The reason…
            My mistakes were made
I then…
            Removed   the   chair   of
despair
From the corner…
            That was dark no more
And my only regret…
            Is that I should have sat
In that corner…
            Long before.

HE

He curls up in a fetus position
In the corner of his room
He knows his life is in HIS hands
And he knows HE'S coming
soon

What will come…
He is afraid to question
But he really wants to know
His only wish is to be set free
Home is where his soul must go

Blame…
He blames no one
It's dark and silent so he cries
His parents fail to heartaches and
pain
And not one single day goes by

Without him…

Regretting   ever   hitting   his
mother
Or ever doing bad in school
He regrets ever trying drugs
I guess everyone has played the
fool

The verdict is in
And it is final
No more…
Waiting in this horrible place

No more…

Being lost and confused
No more...
Heartache and pain
No more...
Sorrowful   expressions   on   his
face

VERDICT

I forgive you my child
You may enter...and yes
I've heard your every cry
Yes, I know you were just curious
I know you did not mean to die

To earn your wings, you must
Watch over your parents
They are in pain
For even owning a gun

You were only eleven when this happened
And you were their only son

Now he is up in heaven
In the most beautiful place
He has ever seen
He knows his life is in HIS hands
Once again, his heart is clean

THE NEXT TIME

The next time it is windy...flow
with the breeze

The next time it rains...cry with
the clouds

The next time it is cold...cuddle
with the chill

The next time it is hot...breathe
softly with the heat

The next time............ may be
your last.

KENT HUGHES

JUST UNDERSTAND

God I'm only asking for an
understanding
The word WHY never crossed
my mind
Some declare this "An act of
war"
While others say "It's a sign of
the times"

Me...
Myself...
I...don't know what to think
But you can believe I gave it a lot
of thought
I wrote what was on my mind...
at the moment
Because there is a lesson that
must be taught

As we watched men on the other
side of the world
Shoot their guns and burn our
flag as they cheered
We found it easy to point fingers
To have someone to blame

But some of the blame may have
started right here

Not the ...
United States
Not the...
Government

252

Not the...
Presidents
Nor the...
Presidents' wives

It started when we stopped
respecting
each other as human beings
Ignoring our brothers' cries

We watched as men, women and
children die
Here at home
And on foreign land
We just changed the channel to
change our minds
Not even trying to understand

We just change the channel
I know I did
As if we were from another
planet

And somehow thinking we're
holier than THOU

Taking each breath of freedom
for granted

It started when we took prayer out of
schools
Not even allowing a moment of silence
It started when we stepped out of
churches and...
Into ...

Hatred Greed and Prejudices

That help fuel this mayhem and malice

The lesson...I don't have to explain right
now
Because we are all feeling about the
same
But when you start pointing fingers,
fingers point back
Yet...we point fingers and use God's
name.

Each day gives us a chance to start over
Let us love each other unconditionally
Let there be peace on earth SOMEDAY
and let it begin
WITH ME

CRACKS FROM THE STONE

Judge my imperfections
Waste your time pointing out my wrongs
Keep missing your beat as you…chastise me
While the drummer is playing…your song
You'll find…
That I'm not that important
You'll see…
The stones hiding in your grass
When you're alone
Seeing cracks from the stones
You'll find…
It's your house that's made of glass

KENT HUGHES

SUNSHINE AND PRAYER

Dark clouds cover the powerless
Sunshine clears the rain
Nighttime ends the daylight
Prayer heals all things

I PRAYED FOR THE CHILDREN

I prayed for the children last night
I asked God to heal their minds
I asked that He give them joy
That only a child could define
I asked that He teach them wisdom
So only righteous…could they say
I prayed for the children last night
That they make it through the day

THE NEXT DAY

The next day
Was a new day
A different day
For the first time I saw the sky
and it was… bluer

The tree line was a perfect cut
I realized the molding of this
world was the image of the Gods
great craft
I thanked God for the epiphany
I praised God for the gift…life

Before the next day
My eyes were tunneled
Open only to what I thought
needed to be seen
What I saw was the darkness of
mans creations
And foolishly became hungry for
the materialistic things

Today…
Is now the next
And I will live for each day
I will breathe with no convictions
I will know that each day is a
precious gift from God
And I will never forget the day
before….
it allowed me to appreciate…
The Next Day

MOVING MY MOUNTAIN

Battered...but not broken
Fragile...yet concrete
No time for daydreaming
Dreamed already in my sleep
Too many dreams...left uncontested
Too many nightmares when I crash
Don't want anyone moving my mountain
Just move...so I may pass

Face me and you face my shadow
Keep up...I'm in overdrive
Question my life and how I'm living
The answer...I will survive
Staying tired as I keep on moving
Always thirsty for that...cool calm water
Following the footprints placed before me
Keeping each step, I take in order
Claiming my destiny...when I'm praying
Staying true to who I am
Don't want anyone moving my mountain
God has given me the strength to climb

BLEMISHED VISIONS

Humanity moving in migratory
Searching for a place to belong
Blemished visions of dreams gone
sour
Trusting words of a primitive
 song
Heavy-handed mouths speak
politically correct
Premeditated conversation in the
light…while…
Bombs are being dropped on the
cream of the crops
As the illustrious loosen tongues at
night

The leaders stepped up to the plate
The uninformed has the ball in
their hand
The underprivileged watches as
leaders play gods
While the oppressed are treated
less than human

Hate mongers are kept top secret
The devils are turning us gray
Reprehensible feeling doused in
fear

They're going to kill us all
someday

The blind mimic the sound that
leads them

4th SUNDAY

The strong thrashes ideas at the
weak
The ignorant being tortured by the
ghost of hope

Blemished vision in dreams as t
hey sleep

MY CRY FOR HUMANITY

I have smothered my tears with my pillow
Fisted each emotion tight
My joys came in the morning
My sorrows came at night

My dance was one of strength
My music was rejoicing…yet silent
My world was one of peace
The reality…peace made through violence

My heart is vast and limitless
My body is of earth and sand
I will lean on the everlasting arms
Yet…why can't we all understand that…
If no tears are shed for our brothers
And wealth is only gained from the poor
Then the future that holds humanity
Is a future that is…no more

Again…

I smothered my tears with my pillow
Hiding puzzle pieces of my sorrows
Surviving the dust of this destruction
Believing in a better tomorrow

My song is one of love
No words just a train of thought
My world is one of dreams
The reality is…hate is taught

My soul prepares for Heaven
My mind is of God and faith
I will follow the path of righteousness
Only a few know He who is Great

For if no hands are together in prayer
And each man tries to walk alone
Only will the few find Heaven
And Hell is earths' eternal home

BLACK FRAME PROVERBS

When you listen to the words of others and what others think about you, sometimes you can do a clear evaluation of yourself.

Sometimes others know you better than you.

To be born in poverty is to understand hunger, struggle, and pain. To be born in wealth is to never understand how to truly pray and be thankful.

Sometimes an ungrateful blessing is a curse.

When you reach for the stars, you are just exercising. But when you reach inside yourself, the stars are the limit.

Sometimes you find the best inside you.

If you take everything to heart, does that leave you any space? Why not take what you need and give your heart space for you.

Sometimes, what others say can help you; it depends on how you take it, how much of it you use, and how much of it you throw away.

FEELING ME
(A letter to the reader)

When you are feeling someone
You tend to feel their happiness
The happiness that captures the very
Essence of what is beautiful about them

And all you can wish is that, the
Someone you feel, only knew how much
You are really feeling them

When you are feeling someone
You tend to feel their pain
The pain that claws at their heart
Like a ferocious lion in a cage of hurt

And all you can wish is that the
Someone you feel only knew how much
You are really feeling them

When you feel someone
I mean-really feel someone
Then you're really feeling me

Ya feel?

AUTHOR'S NOTE

Kent Hughes is a native of Camden, North Carolina. He spent nine years in the United States Army as an infantryman. He is married and has three daughters two sons and one granddaughter. He had the pleasure of growing up in a large family consisting of his loving mother and father, two brothers, four sisters, Kent being number five.

Kent credits his experiences for his desire to express himself through writing. The military can bring a sense of loneliness for home and family. He found himself scribbling on cold late nights in Sinai, Egypt, while he was on a multi-national peace keeping mission. He considered his efforts as something to pass time until the morning. Growing up in a large family taught him how to share and appreciate an unbreakable bond. His children and wife have taught him the true meaning of unconditional love.

How he developed his book was quite interesting. The thought occurred on Thanksgiving Day. He came up with the idea to frame his poetry and give it to family members and friends for Christmas presents. But after several people read a few selected poems, he was told that this would be an injustice to his invaluable work. I suggested that he, instead, should write a book of poetry. Kent being the person he is, wanted a second opinion and asked a very opinionated Yolanda Herring, his co-worker at the time, and she totally agreed with me. Since the frames were black that enclosed his poetry, he appropriately entitled his book Black Frame.

Black Frame was then broken down into different subjects or frames, and the rest, well like they say... is history.

By Shelia Hughes Williams

SMILE